Pulak Kumar

INDIA • SINGAPORE • MALAYSIA

ISBN 979-8-89067-603-0

Contents

Preface

I'd like to thank my friends, family, and the wonderful world of entertainment for inspiring me to write this story down. As I've grown older, I've been intrigued by how different people can be, and how one man's success can be seen as another man's tyranny. The winds of change blow ever onward, and it's easy to question who among us is doing the right thing. Nonetheless, it is an enticing thought that true love can shine even in the face of these uncertainties, and that's the sentiment I've sought to explore in this novel.

By Your Side

She chose to pursue me.

At that point I was still in my final year of university, uncertain of the direction I wanted to take with my life. She, on the other hand, despite being only a year older, already seemed incredibly driven and self-assured.

"So you're Jaina, right?" she said, extending her hand. "I'm Alex. Alex Vander."

"Uh, yeah, hi." I smiled awkwardly and returned the handshake, more out of politeness than anything else. "I've heard of you. You're a trainee at Stellaris Corp's security division, right?"

"That I am," she said. "So, how are you finding your field study here?"

"A little early to tell. Still getting a feel for the place."

As part of our final semester thesis, everyone in my class had been tasked to do a field study at a corporation or non-profit of our choice. I ended up picking Stellaris Corp mainly because I was a little slow on the uptake and all the other options on the menu got snatched up. Not that Alex needed to know.

"Yeah, I get that," she said. "I did get a brief on Gale University's plans when we got picked as an option, and from what I understand your assignment's pretty open-ended. It must be a challenge trying to figure out how to make sense of it."

"It is," I said, deciding there was no harm in being frank. "But I think I'll manage."

"I'm sure you will," Alex said, and then she took a seat beside me. "But I would like to help you out. Mind if I tag along?"

"Are you sure? Don't you have other commitments?"

"Well, as it happens, being a trainee is pretty open-ended too." Alex smiled cheekily. "I've basically been given free rein to understand the organization and take up assignments as I see fit. So, you see, I'm not just helping you out. I'm also helping myself."

"Well, in that case, why the hell not?" I said, returning her smile. "Welcome aboard, Alex."

The two of us clicked almost immediately. I could tell that Alex really did enjoy my company as she showed me around the place, and I couldn't help but be taken in by her infectious enthusiasm. I saw a girl full of passion and confidence, someone who may not know exactly what she wanted, but was nonetheless determined to make something of herself.

She was also someone I deeply envied. Though I had managed to work my way into what was widely considered a fairly prestigious higher-education program, I was for the most part going through the motions, still unsure of where I wanted to end up, and terrified of thinking about it. For all I knew, I could graduate and end up with nothing to show for it, which would be a terrifying position to be in.

At the beginning of the field study project, I put on a cheery, unflappable front. It was never easy for me to open up to strangers or new acquaintances, and many of my relationships had been shallow and transactional as a result. Though Alex was a fun girl to be around, I expected my time with her to end the same way.

That is, until she saw right through me.

It was about halfway into my final semester when she made a demand of me completely out of the blue. She wanted me to share a draft of my report with her.

I was utterly baffled that she would ask this of me, given that she'd seemed so easy-going until now. Or at least, that's what I'd wanted to believe.

The truth was that the signs were always there. She'd noticed me dodging her questions when they got too personal. She'd noticed me looking at her with jealousy as she bragged about moving up in her career. And she knew that I would never give her a straight answer whenever she tried to understand me better.

So this was her way of putting me on the spot. Her way of forcing the difficult conversation of how I was keeping her at arm's length.

And sure enough, when she did see my report, she used it as a pretext for what she really wanted to talk about.

"I'm disappointed, Jaina. This looks so ... generic. Like, facts and figures you could get out of any online search. Canned, uncritical statements about Stellaris without any further examination. Come on, you can do better than that!"

"It's just a first draft," I said. "I'll revise it later."

"Well, even if you do, I don't think it'll reach its full potential with the way you're doing things now," she said. "I've noticed a pattern in your way of working, Jaina. You're treating this whole assignment like a glorified checklist. Just trying to tick off a bunch of boxes without really thinking about what you're trying to accomplish."

"Come on, that's not fair, Alex."

"Oh, I disagree. I think I'm being very fair, and more importantly, accurate, in describing your approach. I mean, I get that you need to do this for your graduation, but this can be so much more than that! I want you to be brave, Jaina! This is a golden opportunity for you!"

"An opportunity for what? Finding out the meaning of life in a fucking megacorporation?!"

Alex looked at me in shock. I too, was horrified at my outburst.

"Oh my God, Alex, look, I'm so sorry, I didn't mean to –"

"Relax." She smiled and gently held my hand. "I'm not mad at you."

"But still, this was so unprofessional of me, and –"

"Tell you what, Jaina? How about you stop caring about being 'professional' around me? This front you're putting up is part of the problem."

"Problem?"

"Yes. I've been watching you over the past few weeks. And I think you've been holding yourself back, Jaina. You're too concerned about getting everything right, ticking off all the boxes and meeting everyone else's expectations of you. But that's not what I care about. That's not why I became friends with you."

"Then why? Why did you?"

"Because I see someone beautiful in there. Beneath all the self-doubt, the apprehension and the fear, I see a girl who can really, truly shine, Jaina. And I don't want that girl to wither away, to just become a puppet of everyone else's agendas. I want you to be free."

"Alex, I ..."

"It's okay. You can take your time with this. Living up to your full potential is a process. It'll take time, and it'll take work. But I believe in you, Jaina. I know you can matter. And I want to be there, by your side, when you make it happen. Will you let me in?"

"I ... I will. I'm so glad you care about me, Alex. Thank you." I smiled, as I felt my chest tighten up. I hadn't planned on it, but Alex had left me defenseless. Vulnerable. And it was one of the best days of my life.

We tore apart the draft I'd prepared and began a new one from scratch. And less than a week later, we kissed each other for the first time and began to date.

As time went on, Alex became a more and more inseparable part of my life. She was always there, guiding me, comforting me, pushing me. By the time the semester ended and I submitted my final report, I was head over heels for her. She was the first person I called up to share the good news with when I finally got my grades and was cleared for graduation.

And that night, we celebrated by getting dinner together, just the two of us. And I could tell where things were headed almost immediately when I saw her in that alluring black dress.

When she broached the matter of us making love to each other for the first time, I accepted without hesitation.

I moved in with her less than a month later. There were so many unanswered questions in my mind, but I knew that I wanted Alex by my side as I worked my way through them. As much as she'd said that she wanted me to be free and whole, I couldn't imagine carrying on without her. She had become so irreplaceable as the woman who held onto me at night, who listened to all my fears, and who helped me past my doubts.

Alex didn't complain. She indulged my neediness without any hint of annoyance or frustration. Even when I felt that I was imposing too much on her, she reassured me that she would always be there for me. That she would always believe in me.

And to my amazement, I did slowly become stronger. More resolved. More conscious of what I wanted out of my life.

I noticed that beneath the comfort and privilege I'd been raised in, lay a brutal, horrific world where a minor misfortune could doom someone to a harsh, unforgiving existence. There were so many people utterly left out in the cold to fend for themselves because the powers that be did not deign to care.

But I could change that. I could use my power to help them.

I joined the Lightwardens, an independent militia and support group dedicated to improving the conditions of the downtrodden. They served as peacekeepers to impoverished areas, and in fact offered a lot of non-combat related support as well, such as ferrying supplies and negotiating with corporate security teams.

I was so happy when I surprised Alex with dinner and broke the news to her.

But her reaction conveyed to me, in no uncertain terms, that life could never be so simple.

"You joined the Lightwardens?" she said, sounding shocked and agitated. "Didn't you know they've been stonewalling the expansion efforts I've been tasked with coordinating? Why didn't you consult with me?!"

That reaction single-handedly took the wind out of my sails. I didn't know how to respond.

Of course I wasn't aware of any hostilities between the Lightwardens and Stellaris. Nothing like that was ever mentioned in my job description, and Alex didn't talk about her work all that much anyway. I was aware, however, that by joining the Lightwardens, I would be butting heads with corporations every now and then, but wasn't that all for the greater good? I didn't know it'd affect Alex so personally!

"Alex, I'm sorry, I didn't know. I just ..."

"No," she said, cutting me off. "No, I'm sorry, Jaina. I shouldn't have acted out like that. The Lightwardens have been causing me a lot of trouble back at my job, it's true. But ..." She smiled and caressed my cheek. "That's no excuse for me to rain on your parade. I know the people there believe they're doing the right thing. That's why you joined as well, isn't it?"

"Yeah, it is. Alex, I ..."

"You don't have to explain yourself to me. You are your own woman, aren't you, Jaina? That means that sometimes you'll make choices that other people, even those you love, may not take so well. But so long as you believe you're doing the right thing, don't let anyone, not even me, convince you otherwise."

I held her hand. "I just don't want to hurt you, Alex."

"I know you don't." She lowered her voice to a comforting whisper, the way she often did when she saw me getting stressed out. "Again, I'm the one who should be apologizing. Now that I think about it, this is what I've always wanted from you. Taking bold action, deciding to make a difference. This is what it means to live to your full potential."

"Okay." I was still in tears, but I could smile through them now. "Thank you, Alex."

I kissed her hand. "And since you're apologizing, I want you to make it up to me. Comfort me, okay? I'm going to make full use of you tonight."

"I'd be happy to, Jaina," she said, as she leaned in for a kiss.

But that night, even though the sex was sweet, and Alex was so loving and warm as she held me, I still couldn't completely erase my memory of the anguish I'd seen in her eyes. I couldn't let go of the fact that I had hurt her, even though she had said that doing so would be inevitable as I became my own woman.

I still took solace in the fact that ultimately, she wanted me to be free. She wanted me to be happy. But I could feel the doubt stirring within me. The very same doubt that Alex had tried so hard to free me from.

Throughout our relationship, I'd been the more needy one. Aside from the emotional support Alex had provided for me, she also owned the house that we lived in and earned far more at Stellaris than I could ever hope to earn working for the Lightwardens. And aside from the occasional offhand comment, she never made any mention of the tensions between Stellaris and the Lightwardens and went out of her way to be supportive towards me.

My time working for the Lightwardens, as well as my increasing awareness of this world, had made me rather resentful of the disproportionate control corporations held over our city-state. They had a long history of manipulating and even overriding governments to serve their own agendas, and their private militaries would often muscle their way into domination when merely signing checks would not work.

Alex, by virtue of becoming Chief of Security at Stellaris, was perpetuating a lot of what my colleagues at Lightwardens would consider thuggery, and even borderline terrorism.

Of course, I strongly disagreed with those assessments, mainly because I wouldn't dare question Alex's motivations or villainize her. I saw absolutely no evidence that someone like her would ever knowingly want to hurt innocent people.

And yet even though I had the utmost faith in her intentions, I couldn't deny that Stellaris was causing considerable harm to the marginalized in practice. They were incredibly aggressive in acquiring lands to mine them for minerals, or for constructing proving grounds for their newer technologies. And this land was often seized from dwellers trying to eke out a modest living.

I never allowed my judgment to be clouded by irrational outrage, however. The truth behind a lot of these problems was immensely complex, and often the best of intentions couldn't compensate for the harsh realities of this world. So whenever I did critique Stellaris when talking to Alex, I was sure to be respectful and open-minded in the way I put things.

Alex recognized my restraint, and often praised me for it. She was in fact subjected to much harsher and unsympathetic variations of my criticisms on a regular basis, so talking things out with me actually allowed her to consider the substance of the issue without feeling defensive or combative.

"I'm so lucky to be with someone like you," she whispered one night, as we cuddled together after a particularly satisfying romp. "You keep me grounded, Jaina. You keep me sane. No matter what I have to deal with, I know I can talk it out with you if I need to. That means so much to me."

"Thank you." I smiled and felt a tear run down my cheek. "I've leaned on you so much all this time. To know that you can lean on me too, it feels wonderful, Alex. It really does."

She gently wiped the tear off my cheek and kissed down my neck. "I love you so much, Jaina. I want to stay like this, forever."

"Yeah." I smiled. "Forever and ever. Just the two of us."

I could see myself becoming more and more her equal, more dependable, more kind. It made me so happy.

"I want to stay with you," I whispered. "For the rest of my life. Marry me, Alex."

"That's just a formality," she said. "As far as I'm concerned, we're already bound for life, Jaina. As partners, in every sense of the word."

"I know. But I want to commemorate it. Make it memorable."

"Sure, we can do that." She smiled as she kissed me on the lips, and we drifted off to sleep in each other's arms.

We never did get our grand wedding, though we did become legal wives for practical reasons when I failed to secure health coverage when working for the Lightwardens. The second I told Alex, she rushed me over to the courts and got us married, and the next day changed her health plan at Stellaris to get me covered.

Part of me did wonder if there was some sort of conflict of interest at play because of this, but Alex emphatically told me not to worry. She said that when push came to shove, I would always come first for her, and I trusted her. I believed her.

It was on our third anniversary that Alex finally followed through on her promise to make our relationship memorable. She told me to come to the nearby amphitheater, but I had to be there alone. She'd go on ahead to make "preparations" and we'd only see each other when they'd been "completed".

So I spent most of the day alone at home, pondering over what she was planning, until the appointed hour came and I drove on over, still clueless.

As soon as I walked into the theater, I saw the lights dim, and a spotlight shine on me. And that's when I saw it.

A majestic figure in imposing armor walked towards me, the face cloaked, and its voice booming and harsh in tone.

"The princess has arrived! And so I must declare to her my oath!" it screamed.

"Princess, what princess?" I muttered in shock, and as if to answer my question, the figure in armor whisked me into its arms and flew me out of the amphitheater.

"Hey! Hey, let me go!" I screamed in panic, but the figure replied in a low, soothing voice. "Do not be afraid. I will never let any harm come to you. Protecting you is my solemn vow. My one oath above all else."

It was then that realization dawned on me.

"Alex, is that you?"

"Indeed, it is I! Alex, the knight of Vander, here to serve you!"

Alex flew me over to the surrounding city, all the while breaking into a grandiose monologue.

"Only a beautiful world could have given rise to a princess as fair as you. But where there is beauty, there is also decay. Where there is love, there is despair. Only by protecting what is beautiful can we hope to rise above the horrors that surround us. Only by nurturing and caring for my princess, can I truly find my purpose in this world."

Alex flew me back into the amphitheater and set me down. She then knelt before me.

"And so I swear to protect and care for you princess. Now and forever. On my oath as a Vander, I promise that I will be your faithful knight, always by your side."

It was then that the mask she was wearing got retracted, and I got to see her smile. Her smile which was so reverent, so devoted ... all for me.

I had my knight in shining armor. Right here and now. This was her gift to me. Her idea of making this moment memorable.

She took my hand in hers, and it felt cold because I was holding steel. She then rose and pulled me in for a kiss.

And that didn't feel cold at all.

"Happy anniversary, my love. My princess."

"Alex, I ..."

I could feel the contours of her armor as she held me close and kissed me again. It wasn't bulky, but I still felt the coldness of the steel, the firmness of its strength. This was no mere costume. This was the real deal.

She didn't give me much room to speak, hungrily kissing me over and over again. I didn't mind, although it certainly was a little tiring to be closely embraced by an armored figure. I could feel the weight pressing down on me.

Finally, Alex stopped indulging herself and pulled back, her face wearing an expectant smile. "So, how was it?"

"It ... it was amazing. I never thought you'd go this far, Alex. And all this ... just for me. Thank you so much!"

"I was just affirming my duty to you, that's all," Alex said, with a warm smile. "Did you know that knights of Vander were a real thing?"

"Huh? Really?"

"Yup. I'm descended from a long line of knights from the medieval and Victorian eras. They were tasked with protecting the nobility and royalty of their lands, with their lives if need be. Of course, stories of love between the knights and princesses were more frequent in chivalrous legends than in real life, but I'm happy to say that our love story is very, very real Jaina."

"I know. I know it is. I love you so much!" I said, and this time I was the one who pulled her in for a kiss.

This was so amazing! She did all of this for me! Recounting her family history, going back to her chivalrous roots, even bringing this fancy suit of armor!

Wait, a suit of armor ...?

That's when it hit me.

"Hey, Alex," I said, pulling back. "This armor. Where did you get it?"

"Oh ..." her exuberant smile faded. She knew what I was getting at, didn't she?

"They're ..." she stammered, immediately losing the showy eloquence she'd been displaying. "This is armor for our new elite ops team. It's a team I'm heading."

"Elite ops ... what for?"

"Tensions have been on the rise, Jaina. Stellaris is planning something major, and for that we need all the resources we can get. And unfortunately, that means we're under pressure too. We can't keep letting all these militias stall us anymore."

"B-but Alex, then ..."

"Hey, I know." She pulled me in for a hug. I knew she was trying to calm me down, but I didn't feel calm. The cold steel of her armor only heightened my anxiety. "I'm not saying we're going to mow them down, okay? That's not what Stellaris does. That's not what I do. But the stakes are high, Jaina, and we need to take decisive action. This elite unit will be a show of strength, and I can negotiate a lot from a position of strength. You understand me, don't you?"

"Alex, were you going to tell me, if I hadn't noticed?"

"I ... I don't know, Jaina. I just wanted to impress you for our anniversary and give you something to remember. But I meant every word of my oath. Every word of what I said. That's all that was on my mind, I swear to you."

"I know, Alex. I know." I felt my fears melt away as I smiled and kissed her. "I know you love me. I know I'm your princess. And I know that it's a knight's duty to protect the realm no matter how hard it gets. That's why I'm worried about you. As any princess would be."

"Jaina ..."

"Alex, I know how hard it must be to be a knight. I know the burden of your duty is immense. That's why I have one small request for you, as your princess."

I caressed her cheek.

"Don't let it become too much, okay? I'm glad you're protecting me, but I don't want to lose my precious knight out in battle. No matter what. The moment it becomes too dangerous, the moment you can't handle it anymore, I want you to come right back to me. I'd be so sad if I couldn't see my knight again. I don't know if I'd be able to take it, Alex!"

"Jaina ..." I could hear her voice crack. "I ... I promise you! No matter what happens, I will always come back home to you! You don't have to worry about being alone! I'll never leave you alone! Never!"

She was crying now. This was the first time I'd seen her cry. For so long, she'd been the one to comfort me. The one to bear my burdens. Even now, she'd vowed to be the knight who would protect me.

But right now, as of this moment, it was my turn to care for her. To bear her burdens.

To be the princess she could lean on.

Love was just as much about enduring the bad times as it was celebrating the good. I really couldn't describe what I had with Alex in words. It wasn't that she always made me happy. It wasn't that she always made my day better.

But I now knew that even with all the hurt and pain she put me through, that I put her through, we wouldn't have it any other way. Because we cared about each other in a way that we never could about anyone else. That was a truth that I did not expect to ever change.

And so it was that even in the face of the greatest betrayal I had ever faced, I would still never leave her side.

It happened two years into our relationship. While my time with Alex was in many ways more fulfilling than ever, my professional life as one of the Lightwardens was falling apart. The federal and local laws were increasingly being weighed against our operations, forcing us to relinquish hard-won victories as corporations continued expanding their hegemony. While Stellaris was turning out to be our biggest adversary in this regard, they were far from the only ones.

More and more communities were lost to oligopolies where they found themselves at the mercy of corporations that had agreed to mutually split territories between them. In fact, Alex had been a major proponent of these oligopolies, arguing that they minimized the need for violent takeovers, and frankly, I agreed with her. Seeing her conscience ease up during our nights together was the biggest comfort I felt in these times. Even if I was losing my own battles, as long as Alex was staying strong, I hadn't lost everything.

Alex never truly bought into my cynicism about corporate intentions. She firmly believed that Stellaris was fundamentally a force for good, and that the people in charge meant well. Though that did mean that she would never turn against her employers, it also meant that she remained incredibly open to my feedback, no matter how harsh it got. She consistently gave me credit for providing her with a fresh perspective that she could then report to her superiors, even though I couldn't shake my cynicism about how much of it would be seriously considered.

Nonetheless, I agreed with her point that neither of us could truly know what the people in power believed. It was perfectly okay for one of us to believe the best of them, and the other to fear the worst. The world was full of these ambiguities, so you couldn't really draw a line in the sand about these matters.

Alex was also incredibly considerate in recognizing that I needed to lean on her once more, and she frequently threw across opportunities my way that I could latch onto in the event my time with the Lightwardens truly fell apart. It did sort of wound my idealistic pride to consider becoming another corporate worker after spending so many years pushing back against them, but I couldn't fault Alex for her sincerity.

"We need to go on vacation," she said one night, as we cuddled together.

"Huh?" I said. I was feeling rather drowsy, and close to drifting off to sleep.

"We need some time away from everything, Jaina." She caressed my hair and kissed me. "I think it's times when the world gets too crazy that you really need to pull back. Get some perspective. There's just so much chaos just waiting to suck you right in, you know?"

"Yeah, you're probably right," I said and brushed my cheeks against her breasts. "But where would we go?"

"I haven't thought that far. But when we do go, we'll disconnect. No wi-fi, no work emails, none of that crap. It's just going to be me, you, and the breeze. And when we come back, the world will still be there. None of these great big problems matter as much as we think they do. What matters is how we take care of ourselves and each other."

"You're right," I said, kissing up her neck. "As long as we can keep snuggling like this, I'll always have hope. You're my hope, Alex. I love you."

"I love you too." She smiled and kissed me as I drifted off to sleep.

I really wanted that vacation, but for the next week, Alex made no mention of it. She seemed increasingly preoccupied, and I was getting somewhat frustrated that she wouldn't be clear with me as to what was going on.

At the same time, the Lightwardens had grown increasingly tense. One of the settlements under their protection had just retaliated against corporate pressure, though a lot of the details weren't clear. Nonetheless, upper management had decided to fully support this settlement's efforts, and I understood their reasoning. If we couldn't protect vulnerable people when they needed us most, who could we protect? We knew that the system was rigged against us, but we had to fight back. Whichever corporation it was.

It seemed a good way to channel my frustration as well. All this time, I'd seen the people in power turn against us, marginalize us and essentially try to exhaust us into giving up, and the most supportive voice I'd come across was herself a corporate loyalist. I absolutely hated the idea of confrontation, especially given my relationship with Alex, but if a gentle approach would get us nowhere, I was ready to push harder.

That is, until I learned just what it was I'd gotten myself into.

That day, like every other in the week, Alex said she'd be working late as she kissed me on her way out. I'd been instructed by the Lightwardens to stay at home and stand by. Apparently, it was getting rather dangerous since a corporate security team was about to make their move. By keeping more of us at home, the Lightwardens wanted to minimize making targets out of us.

Then I got the call.

"We're under attack!" Johan, my commanding officer yelled. "All units, mobilize in defense of the settlement! We're getting rounded up. Those who resist are getting shot! This is an emergency!"

An abject terror seized me. Never in all my years of working for the Lightwardens did I ever anticipate getting mobilized. I'd deliberately avoided the front lines when picking my assignments. I'd wanted there to be room for me to tend to this home. To spend time with Alex. I had resolved, from the very beginning, not to let this work consume me. It was something I took great pride in, as it allowed me to help Alex out of her obsessive tendencies.

But none of that mattered now. The one situation that I'd feared for the most, but never ever believed would come to pass, had happened. I was being mobilized.

There was no time to think. The future of the Lightwardens, of the people I was protecting, was at stake!

I loaded up my firearm and got into my car, heading straight for the coordinates they sent me. I had my gun loaded with rubber bullets, of course, since the thought of taking another life still horrified me to no end. Nonetheless, I could switch my chamber to live ammunition with the press of a switch if it came to that.

I dearly hoped it never came to that.

As soon as I reached the destination, I could see that a war had broken out. And the Lightwardens were being hopelessly overrun.

I ran up to the collapsed bodies and checked on them. They were wounded, paralyzed, but most of them weren't dead, or anywhere close.

Most, but not all.

Two corpses lay in front of me. Once man, and one woman. I could see their arms had been blown off, still clutching the steel knife and pre-21st Colt Revolver respectively. Lethal arms.

"It's over ..." I heard one of the men cry. "They overran us! It's all over!"

Anger burned up inside me as I grabbed my gun and marched forward to survey the scene. But that anger quickly turned to despair as I heard the gunfire die down and the smoke clear.

"All targets down!" I heard a voice say. "Sweeping for stragglers."

Stragglers?! That would include me, wouldn't it? What would they do to me if they saw me? Would I get shot too? Lie down on the ground in agony, like –

"Don't move a muscle," a figure yelled as it pointed its weapon at me. A figure ... in combat armor.

No ...

"Back off!" I pointed my gun at it. "Back the fuck off!"

No, it couldn't be them, this couldn't be happening!

"Lay down your weapon, or I will shoot!"

"No ... no it can't ... it can't be ..."

Why? Why did you do this?! HOW COULD YOU DO THIS?!

"Last chance, miss ... oh." The aggression in his voice completely dissipated as he seemed to recognize me.

"Go away!" I was crying now. The gun was still in my hand but I didn't know where I was aiming. "Go away damn you, go away, go away, go away!!!!"

"Ma'am, I'm just going to take your weapon now. Please, no sudden movements."

"No, no, no, no! You wouldn't, you wouldn't ..."

The weapon was swiped out of my hands in an instant. It was over. It was all over.

All because ... of her.

I fell to my knees and burst into tears.

I didn't know how much time had passed, but it seemed like an eternity to me. It hurt so much. So, so much.

The pain wouldn't go away. Couldn't go away. Not after what she'd done to –

"Jaina!"

"Huh?" I looked up, and there she was. Still in her armor but unmasked. Her look was only that of concern.

"Hey, are you alright, babe?" She knelt and reached for me, but I flinched and crawled back.

"Jaina, I ..." She seemed at a loss for words for a bit, then extended her hand. "Come on, get up. I'll explain everything, but you need medical attention right now."

"Why, Alex? Why ... why did you...?" The tears were still clouding my vision.

"Commander, should we tranquilize her? I think she's too unstable right now."

"No," she said firmly. "No tranqs. She'll come around, let's be patient."

"Oh, Alex ..."

"Hey." Her voice was a whisper now. That whisper, whenever she wanted to calm me. Comfort me.

"I know, alright? I know how this looks. And we will talk, Jaina. I promise you. But let's get you checked up, alright?"

"Damn it, Alex! Damn it all!"

"I know, Jaina. I know." Still a soothing whisper. Still trying to comfort me. Even after all this?

"Come on, Jaina. You'll be safe, and we'll discuss everything, alright? Just come with me."

"O ... okay ..." I said, and took her hand.

There were no physical injuries, though the EMT did recommend I be further examined for signs of PTSD. The on-site psychiatrist could not come to a conclusion, but I stabilized soon enough that I was allowed visitors.

It was strange, waiting all alone in that dark room. I felt like absolute rubbish, but I didn't want to leave either. I didn't want to face the truth, even though it was burned within me.

I'd stopped keeping track of time. I had no idea what time of day it was.

That is, until the door opened, and she came in.

Alex Vander. The commander of the Stellaris team that mowed down the Lightwardens I'd been working with.

I'd figured it out, of course. That's why it was so painful. That's why the very sight of her brought back the horror. The anger. The tears. The despair.

"Hey, Jaina."

"A ... Alex ..."

"Look, I told you I'd explain everything, and that's why I'm here. I know you've got a lot on your mind, but hear me out first. After that, you can say whatever you want to say, okay?"

I felt defeated. Powerless. Of course, there was no other way to do this.

"Okay," I murmured.

"As you're probably aware, one of the settlements under the Lightwardens' protection retaliated against Stellaris earlier this week. As a result, we decided to quell this uprising by apprehending and dispersing both the residents of the settlement, and any Lightwardens who would come to their defense. The operation was meant to be forceful but with minimal lethal casualties. There were two fatalities, however, among the Lightwardens. They attempted to use lethal force on our agents, and were dispatched in self-defense."

"Self-defense, huh ..." I muttered.

"The original plan was simply to retake the settlement and scuttle the Lightwardens in the process. I was under strict orders of secrecy, and so I couldn't discuss this with you. When I saw you staying at home on the day of the operation, I'd hoped you wouldn't get involved. However, the Lightwardens did issue a mobilization order that we didn't anticipate, and I'm guessing that's why you showed up."

I nodded slowly.

"Aside from the two fatalities, every Lightwarden who was subdued is being given medical attention. While the leadership will be charged under domestic terrorism laws, Stellaris has decided to release all lower-level operatives, including you, without charges. As of this moment, you're free to go, Jaina."

"And what if they did charge me, Alex?" I said. "Would you go along with it? Let them charge me as a domestic terrorist?"

"Jaina, I ... I was the one who negotiated with the board. Their original plan was to make an example out of all of you, but I pushed back. I wanted to minimize the number of people who got hurt in all this. They wouldn't budge on charging the leadership, but at least I got to protect everyone else! At least I got to protect you!"

"Protect me?!" I spat. "You killed two of my comrades! You ran us all over with riot pellets and batons because we dared to stand up for the little guy! You call that protection?!"

She didn't seem too shocked at my outburst. I could tell she fully expected it.

"I know, Jaina. I know what I did was harsh. Brutal, even. And I'm not asking you to forgive me. I've even made arrangements for you to get your own housing until you can get back on your feet. I know you care for the people who lost their homes, the people you were trying to protect. But I have to look at the bigger picture. I have to understand the consequences of letting these acts of rebellion slide."

"Yeah, of course, you need to look out for your precious well-meaning megacorps!"

"It is hard to sympathize with them after what just happened, isn't it?" She smiled ruefully. "I'd be lying if I said it didn't bother me how aggressive they are. How quick the board is to crush their opposition. How so many people in Stellaris seem proud of flaunting their wealth at the expense of others. But I didn't stick with this job because I condone any of that, Jaina. I stuck with it because I truly believe that Stellaris is our best hope despite it all."

"How?"

"We're providing order to this world, Jaina. You and I both know that with so many people having such divergent agendas, anarchy is inevitable unless we can prioritize things. Someone needs to step up to the plate and decide what truly matters and what doesn't. And I don't think there's anyone out there who can excel at such a responsibility all the time. Everyone in power will be flawed, severely flawed even. Stellaris is no exception to that. But when I think about everything the organization has accomplished, what we hope to accomplish, I know we're making lives better, Jaina. I understand that's hard for you to believe right now, but it's true!"

"And that makes all this okay? Driving people from their homes, crushing them when they fight back?"

"That's the calculation I have to make as Chief of Security, Jaina. At what point does criticism become enough of a threat to our order? At what point does the spark of rebellion threaten to burn down everything we've worked so hard to build? I believe that what the settlers did this time was a threat to our order. If left unchecked, it would have sparked off a rash of revolts that would've ended in anarchy."

"So if you had another chance, you'd do this all over again?"

"I would."

"Just ... just what was the point of it all, Alex?" I said, breaking down in tears. "You told me to be free, to be my own woman! I chose this path! I chose it, and I trusted you to stand by me! And you took it all away, Alex! You took it all away!"

"I know I've hurt you, Jaina. And I'll always have to live with that. I'll do whatever I can to make it up to you, but I can't abandon my principles. I'm sorry."

"I ... I loved you, Alex! I loved you!"

"And I still love you, Jaina. I understand if you no longer believe me, but I do! I'm not abandoning you, not now, not ever. I'm just ready to accept that you might not want to be with me anymore."

"You ... you'll only hurt me again. You'll tell me I can be my own woman, and then you'll crush me if I go too far. How ... how can I ever ..."

I felt her arms wrap around me as she held me in her embrace.

"No, don't say that." Her voice was cracking. "I ... I never wanted to crush you, Jaina. Please, don't say that!"

"A ... Alex ..."

"I'm sorry ..." She was in tears too. "I tried to keep my cool, to let you walk away, but I can't take this, Jaina! I ... I never wanted to hurt you, why don't you see that?!"

"But you did hurt me ..."

"I know, and I'm sorry! I'm so sorry I put you through this! Even though I saw no other way. But I love you, Jaina. That hasn't changed. Even when I saw you, kneeling, crying, I wanted to make sure you were okay. That's the only thing I care about now."

She kissed me on my forehead and pulled away.

"No matter what you do from now on, I'll keep on rooting for you. I'll support you however I can. Even if you ... rebel against us again, I'll do everything in my power to protect you. I just ... don't want you to see me as your enemy. Is that too much to ask?"

"Y-you're not my enemy, Alex. I know you're not, but ..." I paused and took a deep breath,

"Why does it have to be so hard? Why did you and I have to see things so differently? Why did all this ... all this violence happen, Alex?! And why didn't you tell me? I ... I've been so blindsided ... by everything ..."

"I was just doing the best I could, Jaina. Staying true to my values. Doing right by Stellaris. Maintaining order. I was just hoping you'd never find out like this ... but that was foolish of me. Even if I was sworn to secrecy, maybe I could've done something more to protect you. I'm so sorry I didn't ..."

"Alex, I ..." I wiped my tears but they kept flowing. "This is still going to sting, you know that, right? Even if I stay with you, what you did ... will still leave a mark ..."

"I know, and I'll live with it. I know things can't be the same between us, Jaina. But do they have to be? We're always changing, and growing. And sometimes we fuck up. We hurt each other even when we're trying to do the right thing. But I promise you, Jaina, I will do everything I can to make it up to you, to make sure I don't make the same mistake again. You can stay with me, or you can leave, but I will always love you."

"Yeah ..." I murmured and finally smiled again. "I know you will, Alex."

And I caressed her cheek, and leaned in for a kiss.

She hesitated at first, before returning it, and we lost ourselves in the moment, realizing that we hadn't lost each other at all. We were still here. Our love was still here.

"Thank you," she whispered. "Thank you for giving me another chance, Jaina. I promise you won't regret this."

"I trust you," I said, holding her close. "Maybe not to always make the best decisions, but I do trust you to always care about me. Always look out for me. And I trust that you'll always be true to yourself, and do what you think is right."

"Then I'll do whatever I can to live up to your trust, Jaina. So, how about we go home now?"

"Yeah." I kissed her. "Let's go home."

It took some time for us to fully heal, and indeed things were never quite the same between us. I knew now that Alex was firmly loyal to the corporate hegemony, and while she still respected my feedback and efforts to change things from within, she made no secret that she would put down any efforts to truly dismantle the system as it stood.

For my part, I too made an effort to avoid confrontation as much as possible, and though I didn't end up as a corporate drone, none of the other initiatives I worked on had the ambition or aggression that the Lightwardens did. We had all essentially accepted that Stellaris and their ilk would rule over us.

However, Alex did surprise me with how much more proactive she was being in taking care of my needs. Very rare became the days when she worked too late anymore, and I could see how determined she was to keep coming home and spend some time with me. And on occasions where she did end up cracking down on protests, she made it a point to discuss the entire event with me, asking for my complete, unfiltered feedback, which she forwarded to her superiors.

As a result, some interesting changes did happen. Alex got a lot more autonomy in how she handled her job, which led to a decrease in the brutality of operations across the board, as the more sadistic elements of the security forces were reined in. However, the fundamental purpose of her job never changed, but neither did Alex's fundamental nature as a woman determined to do right as much as she could, so I wasn't too bothered by that anymore.

As for me, while there were certainly limits on the kinds of actions I could push for, there was no filter on my speech. Alex made it a point to support me in that endeavor as much as she could, even when I was viciously critical of Stellaris and other corporations. She never once cracked down on people simply for speaking out, and while that may have been cold comfort to those whose more aggressive revolts were crushed with an iron fist, it was a compromise I was happy to live with.

Alex had a point when she said that the great problems of the world didn't matter as much as how we took care of ourselves and each other. Eventually, the chaos and tragedies that engulfed our society, as well as our roles concerning them, always took a backseat to having an intimate dinner, making love to each other, and basking in each other's warmth as we planned our next getaway.

The world was always there. Shifting, changing, and ultimately impersonal. But I knew now that every moment I spent with Alex was a gift tailor-made just for me. And every moment she spent with me was a gift just for her.

"I think that's what love really is for me," she said as I lay on her lap, euphoric from our lovemaking and snuggling close to her as she played with my hair. "It's the feeling that someone matters to me. And not in a generic, impersonal sense. You matter to me precisely because of who you are, Jaina. The way you look, the way you speak, the values you hold, how it feels to be close to you. All of these add up to you, and that's what is precious to me."

"I understand that, Alex." I smiled. "Looking back on everything I've been through with you, I wouldn't change a thing. Because all these moments are what made you, you. And I will always treasure you, because of who you are."

She continued to pet my hair as she kissed down my neck, and fondled my breasts. This too, was love.

I snuggled closer to her, until I was up to her ears, and whispered, "So let's go on another vacation. Soon." She smiled and kissed me in response. This too was love.

Finally, as I grew drowsy and began drifting off to sleep, Alex whispered to me, in a voice fraught with emotion. "So on my promise of making it up to you, I'm doing well, right? You're happy right?"

I opened my eyes wide open, gently brushed her cheek with the palm of my hand, and said, "I am happy. You're doing amazing, Alex."

That too, was love.

No Conditions

"Was it good?" Alex said, as she gently pushed back my hair, and kissed me on the neck.

"Yeah." I smiled, euphoric from our lovemaking. "It was good, Alex. It was wonderful."

"God, I love you so much." She continued to kiss me and fondle my breasts. Clearly, she still had some energy left in her.

I, for one, was not complaining.

Today hadn't been the easiest of days for me, but Alex was making me forget about all of it. My setbacks. My worries. None of those mattered as long as she was here, comforting me. Protecting me.

My skin was ticklish. My body was warm. My mind was still on a sweet, mellow high. I was smiling as I accepted her kisses.

"Ah!" she moaned, as she finally relaxed and wrapped me in her arms.

"That felt good. That felt so good."

"I'm glad."

"Hmm." She smiled as she continued to caress my hair. "See? If anything's weighing you down, just tell me Jaina. I'll make you feel better just like that."

"I know. This was just one of those days where I somehow forgot I wasn't alone. I lost sight of what I was thankful for. Sorry you had to come all the way over and remind me."

It wasn't as if I'd begged her to leave work early and rush over here. My pride wouldn't have allowed it. But she called me. She checked up on me and saw through the front I was putting up. By the time she made it back home, I didn't see the point of hiding it anymore.

"Hey," she said, cupping my face in her hands. "You love me, right?"

"Of course I do."

"Then I need no other reason to protect you. To comfort you. You can always lean on me. No conditions."

"Yeah." I smiled. "No conditions."

"You need any more help from me? I could stick around, you know? Maybe even use some of my connections to take the pressure off you."

"I appreciate the offer, but it won't be necessary. It was all in my head, Alex. Sometimes I still lose it, you know? Sometimes I can't keep it together."

"Then consider this a safe space for yourself." She kissed me again. "Right here with me, you can be as broken as you need to be. And I'll stay right here, watching over you, until you've put yourself back together."

"Yeah, that'd be nice, Alex. Just stay with me, for some time."

"Okay." She smiled as I wrapped my arms around her. Here, I could be small. Here, I could be needy. And she'd bear it all for me.

Like she had done so many times already.

Hues of Gray

"Jaina?" Alex raised an eyebrow as she saw me waiting at the entrance lobby. "Hey, what brings you here?"

"Hey, Alex." I mustered up my warmest smile and kissed her, but I doubt I did a particularly good job of hiding my nerves, or my apprehension.

"Hey." She smiled back, though I could see the concern coloring her eyes. "What's wrong, love? Everything okay?"

"Yeah, I just wanted to talk to you about something, and I couldn't wait. I know you said you'd have a busy day today, but ..." I reached into my bag and pulled out a folder. "Now I know why."

She took the folder and looked through it, her expression immediately turning grave.

"Where did you get this?"

"An old friend of mine reached out. We knew each other from my time back in the Lightwardens. They told me about this. About what Stellaris, and you, were doing."

"And who was this person?"

"I don't know. Honestly."

Evidently, I wasn't trusted enough to know who they really were, even though they shared this information with me nonetheless. However, I was actually grateful for that. I didn't want to have to choose between the woman I loved, and my friend who was about to expose her company.

Such a direct conflict of interest was more than I could take at this point.

"But you know enough to recognize them as a friend?"

"Yeah, they knew some anecdotes that only an ex-Lightwarden would be aware of, but they didn't say anything that could give a definitive answer about their identity. Not that I couldn't make any guesses."

"No, that's not what I'm asking about, Jaina." She smiled and gently put her hand on my shoulder. "I'm not going to use you for intel on this, that'd be unethical. The fact that you even came to me with this says a lot about how much you care about me, and I wouldn't want to push you into doing anything you'd regret."

"I ... thank you, Alex." I sighed in relief.

She leaned in and kissed me.

"Nonetheless, I suspect this information's going to hit the public soon. I'll have to work with my team and the higher-ups to contain it. Not to mention ... you also have some questions, don't you?"

"Y-yeah, I do ..."

"Okay." She kissed me again. "Go back home. I promise I'll wrap things up here as soon as I can, and we'll talk about this."

"Sure." I kissed her back. "Come back soon, okay? I love you."

"I love you too," Alex said, with a warm smile. She then turned around, and headed back towards her office, while calling someone on the phone.

"We have a problem. Yes, heading your way now ..."

I drove back home and waited for her. Now that I thought about it, there really wasn't any reason for me to be shown what my friend showed me. If anything, it was a risk. They knew I was married to Stellaris's chief of security. They knew that I'd have a massive conflict of interest in handling this information. So why did they do it?

I could only think of one answer: spite.

They called me a friend and reminisced about our time at the Lightwardens, but it was becoming clear to me that they wanted to spite me. To shame me for staying together with the very woman who had dealt the killing blow to our organization. They despised Alex, and now they despised me by association.

It's not like I didn't sympathize with their sentiment. But it was still so cruel. Alex and I, we were just people at the end of the day. We didn't want to be evil, so why were we being treated like such monsters?

I heard the front door open as Alex walked in. As soon as she locked the door behind her, she headed right toward me, her arms wide open.

I accepted her embrace.

"Hey, babe," she whispered as she kissed me on the cheek.

"Hey, Alex." I smiled. It was as if my anguish had just melted away. Because I was in her arms again.

I trusted her. I loved her. And she knew that I needed her right now.

"Come on, let's go to your room." She smiled as she led me by the hand.

"My room?"

"Yeah. You're going to be asking the questions, right? So let's do it on your territory."

"O-okay ..."

As we entered my room, Alex took off her shoes and her jacket and plopped down on the bed, looking relaxed and carefree. Completely unlike someone whose company was about to be put on blast all over the airwaves soon.

"You're so carefree," I muttered as I caressed her face. "How?"

"It's simple. It's because I'm with you," she said and kissed me.

"Oh, Alex ..." I wrapped my arms around her. "You know I love you, right? You know I believe in you, don't you?"

"Of course I do," she whispered. "So ask me whatever you want to. I'll listen to everything you have to say."

"Okay," I said as I kissed her. "So, the documents I got ... you've been doing weapons deals, haven't you?"

"I have."

"The documents they sent me ... there was also a video recording. It shows that you supervised the shipment and handover personally."

"I did."

"And these weapons you've sold ... my friend says that they're going to be used by bad people, that Stellaris is just a war profiteer now."

"I'm not surprised they'd accuse us of that, Jaina. I won't deny the board at Stellaris does find the weapons business highly lucrative, and I won't deny that this business by nature has some dark moral implications. But I chose to stand by my company because I believe our ends still serve the greater good. I'm quite used to being hated, and I know I won't always get things right, but on balance, I truly believe I'm doing the right thing, Jaina."

"Alex ... do you have any say in the kinds of deals Stellaris makes? Don't you have any input at all?"

"Only when it comes to our security. I get the final say when it comes to strengthening our defenses or dealing with direct threats to Stellaris and its properties. But a lot of these weapons deals are made with external parties, for their security purposes. I don't get to make the call on who they are."

"But do you know who does?"

"I do, actually." She smiled and kissed me. "She's a good friend of mine. You'd like her a lot, Jaina."

"And you trust her? You know she's a good person?"

"Yes, I do. I believe she's doing what's best, for the greater good. It's not an easy job, by any means. I don't envy the thorniness of it all that she has to keep enduring. But she's kind, she's intelligent, and she's self-aware. I believe in her."

"Okay." I smiled and kissed her. "If you trust her, then I won't doubt you, Alex. I just ... I just wish there was a simpler way, you know? No matter how you slice it, weapons are tools for death and destruction. Even if you try to channel it, you're still accepting that we must continue to kill each other. That we must continue to be at war."

"Jaina, I ..." She smiled and kissed me, deeply. "That's what I love about you. Your idealism. Your simplicity. If it was anyone else saying all this, they'd have done so with contempt. They'd have already given up on Stellaris, on me, and they would've wanted to tear us down. Which ironically, would just start another war. But you ... I can listen to you and challenge myself. I can listen to you and feel safe even when I don't agree."

She suddenly pushed me down on the bed, and I gazed at her smiling face towering over me.

"That means so much to me, Jaina. You're the only one I can have these conversations with."

She kissed me again. Slowly. Deeply.

"I love you so much. So, so much!"

She was beginning to fiddle with my clothes now. Undoing my buttons. Loosening my belt.

"Alex ..." I said, between kisses. "I want to meet her."

"Huh?"

"Your friend ... who handles the deals. I want to talk to her."

"Oh? So you can question her, then?"

"Yeah, if you're friends with her, then you can get her to trust me too, right? Then maybe, if I understood her, I could try to change things, you know?"

"Hey, if you're that eager, why don't you join us?" Alex said with a giggle.

"Huh?"

"If you want to influence Stellaris policy, why not come work for us? You know I can set you up, right?"

"Alex, we've had this conversation. You know I want to be independent."

"Hey, I'm just saying. We both know that Stellaris is everywhere now. You can't escape it, and you always wind up tangled in our affairs no matter what. So if you want to change things from within, just come work for us! That way, you'd always have a say, day in and day out."

"I don't know, Alex ... would they accept a former Lightwarden?"

"That was a long time ago, babe. As long as you're useful, they won't care if you've acted against them. And I'll vouch for you."

"Alex, I ..." I smiled as I caressed her cheek. "You're always looking out for me."

"So, is that a yes?" She tried to play it off as teasing me, but I could see the excitement in her eyes. She really wanted this for me, didn't she?

That way, I'd be in the same circles as her. I'd have the same goals. She'd never have to worry if our professions ever pitted us against each other.

And it'd be a lot easier for her to introduce me to her colleagues if we all worked together to begin with, right?

"I don't want to get you in trouble. If I run my mouth and cause a scene, then ..."

She cut me off with a kiss.

"You won't. After all, you said it yourself, didn't you? You believe in me. So I know you'll understand. Once you see things for yourself, you'll finally appreciate all the good we can do at Stellaris. You won't need to make a scene."

"Alex, I do believe in you. I trust you. But ..."

"But what?"

She was gently caressing my cheek, a genuine look of concern on her face.

"I ... I don't trust Stellaris. I'm sorry."

"Jaina ..."

"I ... I'm sorry. I'll go wash up, and ..."

"Hey." She grabbed my arm and held on to it, firmly. "That's not how we do things here. That's not how I do things. I don't want you to be afraid of me. Not ever."

"Alex ... you're not mad?"

"Mad?" She kissed me. "Why would I be mad at you?"

"You wanted me to join Stellaris so badly, and I just shot it down. And I know you believe in them, but I still ..."

"Didn't you hear what I just told you, silly?" she chuckled. "I love you. Even when you criticize me, even when we don't agree, I feel safe around you."

She leaned in, and once again kissed me slowly, deeply.

"So what if you don't agree with my suggestion? You're still my precious Jaina. You're still the woman I love. That won't change."

"Oh, Alex ..."

We kissed again.

"So we'll do things your way. I'll invite Becca over, just for a few drinks. A night out. Girls getting to know each other. Then you can strike up a conversation with her, keep it casual. I'm sure she'll open up to you eventually. How does that sound?"

"That sounds great, Alex. Thank you!"

"You're welcome, my love," she said, as she resumed undressing me. "I'm always here for you. Never forget that."

"I'll try not to, but I appreciate you reminding me," I said with a chuckle. "I'm so lucky to be with you."

"I'm lucky too, Jaina." She smiled, as she explored my body. "So let's celebrate each other now."

For the One Who Matters Most

"It's beautiful, Alex. So, so beautiful."

I felt so happy, so grateful that I had someone who would do this for me.

The fireworks lit the sky as Alex held me close to her, the both of us staring out the balcony.

"I'm glad you liked it, Jaina," she said as she kissed me. "But it wasn't just my doing. My friends at Stellaris were instrumental in making this happen."

"They must really like you a lot, huh?"

"I won't deny I've built my share of goodwill," she chuckled. "But I think my friends happen to be a bunch of romantics themselves. I've heard them discussing their love lives and all."

"Oh, okay." I giggled. "And what, you think they might be living their fantasies vicariously, through us?"

"I do. And I'm not complaining." She giggled as we kissed again. "I'll take any chance I get to make you happy, Jaina."

"I am happy, Alex. I'm so, so happy I'm with you."

All this, just for my birthday. The lengths Alex went through to pamper me made me feel so warm and cuddly.

"I ... I'll always remember this. Thank you for loving me."

"Thank you for being part of my life, Jaina." She smiled. It was such a warm smile. "It's all because of you that I still feel like I'm on solid ground, even after all this time. You remind me that I'm human, that I'll always be human. I can't put a price on the gift you've given me."

"Alex ..." I was choking up now, the tears blurring my vision. "I love you. I love you!"

I wrapped my arms around her, as tightly as I could.

"I love you too," she whispered in my ear.

I woke up the next morning facing her as the sunlight streamed into our hotel room. This would be our last day here, before we headed back home tomorrow.

"Hey," she said, as she caressed my cheek.

"Good morning." I smiled as I kissed her and fondled her breasts.

"Hmm, keep going," she muttered. "It feels good."

"Okay."

I was completely lost in the moment, enjoying Alex. Touching her, kissing her, exploring her. And I knew she wouldn't ask me to stop. We had time here. We were free to lock away everything else but each other.

She looked so warm and content when I finally had my fill of her. Shortly thereafter, room service came in with the brunch we had ordered.

"So, I've set up a meeting with Becca and Gabby this evening. You'll get all the time you need to really hash things out with them," Alex said, as we began helping ourselves.

I giggled in response. "Wow. It's a rare occasion where you're the one bringing this serious stuff up. You could've just let me enjoy myself and leave, and I would've been none the wiser."

"Well, I guess I've grown to care too much about you then." She smiled cheekily. "I promised you that I'd help you be heard however I could, and I intend to keep it."

"I know. And thank you, Alex." I kissed her. "I promise you won't regret it."

"Hey, no need to hold yourself back on my account." She kissed me back. "I know you're trying to do what you feel is right, and I know you love me. I have nothing to fear."

"Okay." I smiled as we finished our meal.

We then passed the time just quietly being with each other, talking when we felt like it, and letting our gestures and touches do the rest. It felt so liberating not to have to put up appearances, not to have to put on a front. With Alex, I could just ... be.

When the time finally came to meet Becca and Gabby, I did feel some of my nerves tense up again. Alex hadn't been wrong in how she described them. They had both been incredibly kind and sweet to me all this time, but I also knew that they had important roles to fill at Stellaris.

I already knew that Becca had been at the center of the weapons deals I'd found out about, practically deciding who lived and who died as part of her job. Gabby was an even bigger catch. The Chief of Corporate Strategy, she'd been climbing the ranks pretty quickly, despite facing more and more pushback the further she went.

As much as Stellaris loved to tout their progressive credentials by placing women and minorities in prominent positions, the people on the board were still all men. Gabby had a real shot at changing that, given that the company was planning a restructuring of the top brass, and the CEO had a cordial relationship with her.

This was it. My biggest chance to make a dent in their policies and practices while remaining independent. Earlier on, I would've said that I was doing this for my principles because I knew that so much of what Stellaris was doing was wrong. But my reasons were a lot more personal now.

I wanted Alex to be more at peace. I wanted her to feel safe, to not have to worry so much about the criticism and dissent Stellaris was facing. She was still as loyal as ever and would continue to champion this megacorporation and destroy any opponents they asked her to. But I knew it weighed on her. She still hadn't forgotten her role in destroying the Lightwardens, and what that did to me. She hadn't forgotten my misgivings about Stellaris.

And even though I'd already forgiven her, already made clear that I would love her and believe in her no matter what, this was my chance to go beyond that. I would be Alex's champion. I'd do everything in my power to make sure that the good people at Stellaris felt empowered enough to truly make the company a force for good.

"Hey," Alex said, facing me. "You okay?"

"Oh, uh ..." I looked down at my hand, which was holding hers. Looks like my grip had tightened a little too much.

"Yeah, I'm fine Alex." I smiled and kissed her, letting her hold me as I relaxed my posture. "But thanks for caring."

"Alright, if you say so." She kissed me. "But if it ever gets too uncomfortable for you, you let me know and we'll call this whole thing off. I'm here for you, okay?"

"Okay." I smiled, as she slowly let go of me and we headed for the private bar where they were waiting.

Alex immediately ordered drinks for all of us as soon as I'd said my hellos, in a pre-emptive attempt to break the ice. It worked.

"So, how're you enjoying the little celebration we set up?" Becca said.

"It's ... been amazing. Thank you all for doing this," I said and politely smiled. I did feel a certain hesitation in thanking Becca and Gabby though, like I was being manipulated through my gratitude.

I felt Alex's hand on my shoulder, reassuring me, almost as if she'd read my mind.

"Well, let's not forget it was my idea. You all just followed my lead!" she said, immediately afterwards. Her tone was cheeky, but I got the sense she was trying to take the pressure off me.

"Oh yeah, of course. You have no idea how much Alex micromanaged the whole thing!" Gabby laughed.

"Uh, well, I hope she wasn't too hard on you."

"No harder than we've been on her," Becca said. "After all, at work we're both kind of her seniors."

"And you'd be nowhere without me!" Alex said with a chuckle.

"That is true. She keeps our wheels spinning for sure!"

"So, Jaina, right? Becca and Alex have told me a lot about you. I believe you've had quite the ... history with our organization," Gabby said.

And my insides immediately tightened. Just like that, she'd brought up the elephant in the room.

"I have," I said, looking her in the eye. "There are a lot of ... complicated opinions I have on Stellaris."

"I see." She adjusted her glasses. "And where would you like to start on them?"

"I ..." I gulped. "I won't deny you've all been pretty good to me since the Lightwardens incident. Alex is the breadwinner of our household. I've lived with her in company-sponsored housing, with company-sponsored health insurance. I can't deny I've benefited a lot from Stellaris. I've been quite privileged on balance."

"Privileged, huh?" Becca said, taking another sip.

"Yes. I've been doing well, mainly because I fell in love with the right person. I've had people with power and means look after me and care for me. I've never, ever lost sight of that."

"Hey, Jaina baby," Alex sounded a little worried as she put her arm on my shoulder. "I've told you before, you don't have to -"

"It's fine, Alex. Let me finish," I said. She didn't respond.

"That being said, I'm also aware that my privilege had protected me from the horrors most people in this world, heck, in our own country are facing. Every time I listen to the radio, and tune into my news feeds, I'm reminded of how ... unimportant so many lives seem to be. How people are just straight-up neglected, or treated as pawns in these bullshit power games that make no sense. People outside of my circle ... our circle ... they get manipulated, left to die or just killed off in wars. I can't turn a blind eye to that. And I can't ignore the fact that Stellaris is one of the largest megacorps in this country. You're part of the system. A major part."

"I see," Gabby said, her expression inscrutable. "You know, I've known Alex since before she met you. We joined Stellaris at almost the same time. And ever since she fell in love, I've seen her be happier, more fulfilled, but also ... conflicted. I could tell that every hard decision she made seemed personal to her, and frankly, I didn't understand that at first. Why was she thinking so much of people she'd never met, never known? I can now see that you were the factor that altered her perspective so much, Jaina. Especially after you came into our crosshairs."

"I ... I know I've caused Alex a lot of trouble. She cares deeply about me, and ..."

"Relax, I'm not saying she's in any kind of trouble. This conversation's about you, Jaina, and you don't work for us."

"O-okay ..."

"We're, of course, well aware of the work you did with the Lightwardens and the work you have been doing since. Even though you aren't actively obstructing our operations anymore, you're still a very vocal critic of ours. Obviously, I don't expect you to take up arms against us, or anything of the sort. You know that all of us, even Alex, will stick by Stellaris until the end. That's not out of any sense of blind loyalty, however."

"A lot of what you've said, Jaina. We've thought about it too, in our own ways," Becca said. "We came to this decision after considering all our options. Sticking with Stellaris, this system is what best suits our priorities, both concerning our own lives, and what we want from society at large."

"I understand. I do. And I've made that decision myself. I want to stay with Alex. I want to be a part of your world. Losing the love of my life, losing all the friends I've made and the people I've known, I can't pay that price for any reason, no matter what it is. But until Stellaris changes, really changes, I'll feel like I simply chose the lesser of two evils."

"So you think we're evil, do you?" Gabby looked me in the eye.

"Not in an absolute sense. I would never consider Alex to be a rotten person, and I'd never accuse either of you of being evil either. But when it comes to your organization, the impact it's having on this world, on the people at large ... I do believe Stellaris is a force of harm. Of destruction. I'm not saying that you wanted things to be this way, or that you even have to agree with me, but that's my opinion. My belief."

"Your opinion is not at all uncommon. In fact, I believe you're quite mature for criticizing Stellaris without issuing a blanket condemnation of everyone associated with it. There are so many people who've given up on dialog. Who've already decided that it's either them or us. We could never negotiate with those people, but I can at least talk to you."

"I know. That's why I came here."

"So, Jaina, let me offer my perspective on things. I do believe that Stellaris is ultimately our best bet against surviving and thriving in the current world we live in. We need to not just consolidate our power but expand it. Humanity needs an example to look up to, and an aspirational dream to follow. And they need strong leadership who won't dither about in indecisiveness. Stellaris must do what needs to be done to ensure the maximum benefit to the world on a sustainable basis, even if there are people who end up left out."

"So, you do disagree with me, after all."

"In a sense. You mistrust Stellaris. You probably don't want us to have so much power if you think we've done so much harm with it. But what you don't see is all the damage that could have been done had there been a power vacuum without us. How many problems would've been caused if the elected middlemen we had to bargain with held as much leverage over us. I sense an old-fashioned idealism within you, Jaina. You probably long for the good old days when we had a strong democracy that no corporation could control, don't you?"

"Absolutely. We need a system that's not beholden to short-sighted greed! We need a system that lets the people have a voice!"

"And yet it's the very corruption of that system that led us to where we are today, Jaina. Greed corrupts everyone in power, whether they're elected officials, or corporate honchos. So, isn't it better that instead of eliminating greed, we channel it? Manipulate our intrinsic vices for the greater good?"

"So, that's why all of you believe. That's why you're so loyal to Stellaris ..."

"Indeed, it is. Isn't that right, Becca? Alex?"

They both solemnly nodded in response. For the first time in this entire conversation, I felt alone.

"So that's why you'll continue to pursue profits above all else? And leave the useless people out to die, is that it?"

"Jaina, please, no one's saying that." Alex sounded hurt as she responded, her arm still on my shoulder.

"Alex ... I'm sorry ... but what else am I supposed to think?"

"Jaina," Gabby said. "It's true that there are many people who cast value judgments on the marginalized and the neglected to feel better about their decisions. To feel more righteous in their actions. But that's not what I'm suggesting at all. I won't sugarcoat our actions and dress them up as anything other than ruthless calculus. What ventures do we sacrifice for the sake of more sustainable ones? What compromises do we make to protect the health of our organization? What people will end up neglected while we pursue the best of all possible options? Those are decisions I struggle with all the time, and they're often ugly."

"Then what about me? When do I become too much of a liability? When do I stop mattering to you?"

"Hey!" Alex forcibly shook me until I faced her. "Don't you ever say that! Don't you ever tell me that you'll stop mattering to me, you understand?!"

"Calm down, Alex. I don't think she was talking about you. At least I hope she wasn't." Gabby said. "Jaina, I won't deny that you're a special case. If you ever get tangled up in our decisions, of course we're going to take it personally. Of course we'll struggle with it more, and so we'll try to avoid such a situation. So, you're going to be pretty safe around us. Far safer than someone we don't know."

As I tried to respond, she cut me off. "I know what you're going to ask next. Where's the justice in that, right? Why should we prioritize the people we know, over those we don't? How does that make us any different that a clique, or a cult? The truth is, Jaina, that this is also a reality of human nature. We're intrinsically wired to care more about those close to us, than those who're not. Heck, it's the entire reason you're willing to sit down with us and have this talk. You care about Alex. She's special to you, and she works for us, so it's in your interest to get along with us."

"I know ... I know that ..." I muttered. "But can't you do anything better? Can't you agree to change in any way?"

"We can, but I'm afraid we're not going to operate on your terms, or at your pace. I expect you to remain dissatisfied with us going forward. Know this, however," Gabby said, finally smiling after a while. "We've all had the same thoughts you have. And personally, I both understand you and empathize with you. I can feel the anguish of people who feel let down by us. I know that if I were in their position, I too would be resentful. And strange as it sounds, I'm glad you reminded us of their pain, Jaina. Conversations like these prevent me from getting complacent about our situation. We know we're operating on a delicate balance here. But all things considered, I still believe this system is the best way to be."

"Okay then. I'll just have to keep speaking, and speaking and shouting if I need to. I won't forsake everything Stellaris has given me, but that doesn't mean I'm going to bow down to it."

"Then don't." Gabby's smile widened. "Crushing dissent leaves a poor taste in all of our mouths anyway, even if it sometimes has to be done. Even if we silenced all opposition, the opposition won't stop to exist. So, I promise you this, Jaina. We will never silence you. Even if I don't see eye to eye with you, I trust you. Genuinely."

"Okay then. I guess that's the most I can hope for."

"Alright then, Becca and I have plans for the night. We'll leave you lovebirds to it, then!" she said, her friendly demeanor having completely returned as she and Becca left.

I turned to face Alex.

"So, uh." She smiled awkwardly. "I guess things got a little heated there. I know I lost my cool a little too, and I just-"

I cut her off with a kiss.

"I know you'll never abandon me, Alex. I'm sorry I made you think otherwise." I kissed her again. "And as long as you're doing what you truly believe is right, I will always stand by you. Always."

I held her hands in mine.

"Just promise me you'll always stay true to yourself, okay? And that you'll talk to me if you need any help?"

"Jaina ..." She wrapped her arms around me. "I know you want so much more for this world. So much more from Stellaris. I'm sorry I can't just give it all to you."

"No one can, Alex. No one person can change the entire world. And I wouldn't want you to do anything you don't agree with."

I kissed her.

"The fact that you care, is good enough for me."

"Okay," she said. I could see the tears streaming down her cheeks. "I promise you, Jaina. I promise I'll always be true to myself. That I'll never shut you out."

"I'm glad to hear it," I said as we held each other close. "I love you, Alex."

"I love you too, Jaina."

My Aphrodisiac

"Alex …" I murmured as she ravished me, feeling up my body with a hunger that left me overwhelmed.

"Mmm …" was all she said as she smiled and roughly pulled off my top. I wasn't wearing a bra underneath.

I cupped her face to slow her down, only because I wanted to kiss her myself. She'd pushed me down and was having her fill, but I didn't want to remain passive. I wanted to indulge my appetite too.

"All right." She undid her blouse and guided my hands to her chest. "Your turn."

I smiled and grabbed hold of her breasts, but I didn't stop there. I pushed back, hard, until I was the one on top of her. And then I went all out, fully intent on satisfying myself.

"You've gotten stronger. That was one hell of a push," she said with a giggle. I was too busy indulging myself to respond.

"But I like it when you get rough with me. It's ... refreshing."

I smiled as I heard that and kept up my feast.

"But it's right at the cusp of victory that people let their guard down."

An overwhelming force pushed me from my position, pinning me to the mattress again, as Alex looked down on me, triumphant.

"I win."

"No!"

I pushed back, but she didn't relent. We ended up rolling all over the bed, all the while trying to feed off each other to satisfy ourselves. It didn't take long for our lustful urges to completely take over as we became singularly focused on ravishing each other.

When the euphoric climax finally took over me, I felt so gratified. So happy. So warm.

"Oh, Jaina! AH!" I heard Alex scream. Yes, she felt it too! She was happy too!

"Alex!" I moaned as I buried my face into her chest. We both were completely intertwined as the pleasure, the euphoria, washed over us.

My breathing slowed down as I caressed her body. There was some wetness there, probably from the sweat, but her touch felt so comforting. So safe.

"This was a nice idea, wasn't it?" Alex smiled as she played with my hair. "The excitement of seeing a new place, the romance of a beautiful locale. It really brings the energy back."

"It does. I love you, Alex." I smiled and kissed her. "I'm so happy you brought me here. This was an amazing vacation."

"Was? We're far from done, you know."

"I wouldn't mind if we were. This moment with you is more than enough for me."

"I'm glad to hear you say that." She smiled and kissed me. "But we're going to make many more memories here. Memories that will always be there to remind you how precious you are to me."

"I'm so lucky I have you. I'm so lucky you care so much. So, I'll make the most of my time here. I'll be happy because you want me to be."

"I do. Your smile, your joy is the most priceless thing I've ever known of Jaina. I mean that." She kissed me again.

"I believe you, Alex. I want you to be happy too. And I want you to remember how grateful I am. I'll never, ever forget this."

I caressed her body. It was so warm. I liked the warmth.

"I don't even know how much it would cost to keep a place like this. It's wonderful to be here, even if it's just for a couple of weeks."

"Jaina, about that ..." Alex said, a mischievous glint in her eyes. "I never said we rented this house for a couple of weeks. I said my vacation was for a couple of weeks."

"Huh? Wait, are you ...?"

"That's right. I've already bought this place. It's ours now."

"You ... you're serious?"

"I am." She was beaming with joy as she kissed me. "We can come back here any time we want. The next time city life gets to you, or you want to get away from it all."

She caressed my cheek. "Or when we grow old. When our lives have been spent and there's nothing more for us to do than watch the sunset, together."

"Alex, why didn't you tell me? I could've chipped in, paid my share, and ..."

"Oh, you can pay me back if you want to," she said with a laugh. "But I wasn't going to impose that upon you. Remember what I've said, time and again. No conditions. I love you, and I want to share my life with you. I expect nothing in return. I want nothing in return."

"Alex, I ... could never have done something like this for you. This isn't fair." Without warning, my voice started to crack, and tears started to stream down my eyes.

"And why should I care about that? Why should it matter to me? I love you because you've already given me everything I could want, just by being the way you are."

She wiped my tears.

"My only selfish wish is that I want to keep you. I want to keep treasuring you, pampering you and making you happy. And I can see us being together, Jaina, all the way to the end. Just stay mine, and all of this will be yours."

"Alex ..." I kissed her. "You didn't have to do all this, and still you did ... all because you want me. All because you love me."

I smiled.

"I am yours. I don't plan on going anywhere. I'm so grateful for everything you've done for me."

"We're going to be together, all the way to the end," she said. "And this will be our sanctuary. A haven, just for us."

Alex smiled as she continued to caress my face. "Nothing would make me happier than living my fullest life with you. And if we have each other even in our dying moments, well, I'd be happy to die in your arms, Jaina."

"Well, I guess that sucks for whoever among us outlives the other, doesn't it?" I chuckled.

"No, Jaina," Alex said, her gaze firm, but her smile remaining. "That's what these memories are for. So that we can continue to comfort each other, and inspire each other, even after death. We'll make as many memories as we can so that we won't forget, we can't forget how much we love each other."

"Yeah, but even those can fade away. One of us could have a genetic disease of some sort, neural degeneration …"

"Maybe. No one can account for everything, after all. But isn't it worth it to try, nonetheless?

Isn't it worth it to hope for the best, rather than obsessing over the worst? Isn't it worth it to make the most of how fortunate we are, Jaina?"

"Alex ..." I smiled and kissed her. "Of course it is. I wouldn't trade my time with you for anything. I want to keep loving you day after day. I want to have this sanctuary where it's just us."

I gently traced my hand down her hair. "I'm really, really happy. I love you so much."

"I love you too, Jaina." She drew me closer, until we were entwined again, and I could feel her warmth envelop me. "Always, and forever."

Playmates

"I finally did it!" I said, checking my email. "I made partner! I'm going to be a lawyer now!"

"I'm happy for you." Alex smiled as she held me from behind as she kissed down her neck and fondled my chest. "Well, partially happy."

She turned me around and began to kiss me in earnest. "You do know that fast-track law degrees are meant to encourage corporate lawyers, right? Not activist types who give Stellaris a hard time."

"I'm sorry," I murmured sheepishly, while still kissing her back. "I know you've wanted me to come around for a while now."

"I know, and you keep finding new ways to disappoint me," she said playfully, guiding me to bed. "You began legal training online and gave me no clue about your endgame, you cleared the bar exam, and now that I see what partners you're associating with, I'm surprised it took me this long to get it."

The smile that followed was one of the most voracious I'd ever seen from her.

"And you know what? That totally turns me on."

I giggled as she aggressively pushed me on my back and began undressing me.

"I'm gonna make you forget all about your precious little aspirations. You'll be so overwhelmed by what I have in store for you, you'll never want to leave, sweetheart."

"What do you mean? I already never want to leave you."

"Very funny, Jaina." She smiled as she ravished me. Eagerly. Hungrily. Joyfully.

"You're starting to enjoy this, aren't you? This tension, of loving me to bits even though I'm not completely on your side?"

"You're goddamn right I am! Now shut up and surrender yourself to me!"

"Again, I have nothing left to surrender," I murmured as I felt her hands and lips exploring me. Stimulating me. "I want to be your plaything. I want to be your toy."

I cupped her face and looked right into her eyes.

"I've already accepted being your lifelong lover and partner. You can't take away anything from me."

"Ah, you've got some comebacks on you, huh? Let's see how long you can keep it up once I've finished with you."

It felt good. It felt so good.

"Excitement and pleasure are slowly clouding your mind. Once I'm through with you, all you'll care about is how much you want me. HAHAHA!!"

She laughed like a cheesy villain while eagerly relishing my body. Of course, she was right. I was slowly losing track of everything but her. How gorgeous she was. How excited I was by her every touch. Her every kiss. How I wanted her, and her alone, to please me. Hold me. Keep me.

"I know, but here's the thing Alex." I smiled back. "I don't mind one bit. You've played right into my hands!"

And then I pushed back and let my body speed things up. Just because I wanted what Alex was giving me didn't mean I had to let it all happen at her pace. I too had my hunger. My drive.

My impatience.

"Jaina … AAAAH!" she screamed in ecstasy as I squeezed her breasts, as fiercely as I could. I knew she was happy. I knew she was enjoying this, but I still gave a cheeky smile, as though I'd just defeated a villain.

And then I felt the euphoria seize control of me, and the pleasure was all I could think about. "Alex! Yes, Alex!"

I could see her devilish smile as she buried her face in my breasts.

"Yes, that's right Jaina. No matter what happens, you'll always be mine."

"I … I know. I surrender."

"I accept it." Her voice softened. "And I hereby pronounce your sentence. You will always remain my most precious and beloved companion. You will always be the woman I love. My partner for life, who I will always treasure."

"What can I say, Alex?" I giggled as I kissed her. Slowly. Deeply. "You got me."

Tears

"I'm sorry … I'm so sorry!" I was crying. Alex gently cradled my head in her lap, as she held me closely and gently patted my back.

The unthinkable had happened. Someone had bombed a Stellaris branch office. Becca was there at the time, and she got injured. She was fighting for her life in the hospital right now.

And who'd been the one constantly putting them on blast and fighting them at every turn? Me.

"It's okay, Jaina. Everything's going to be okay."

"No, it's not. I'm responsible. I … I ruined everything!"

"You didn't, Jaina." She kissed me. "You haven't ruined anything. This isn't your fault."

"People were using my writings, my words to … to justify their conspiracy theories. They were going crazy, enabling each other, and I did nothing!"

"There's nothing you could've done."

"I could've stopped. I could've stopped talking and just let things be. I could've just accepted this world as it was like you wanted me to!"

"You did accept it. You accepted me, Jaina. Even with everything you've said, everything you've believed, you've continued to love me." She cupped my face in her hands, and looked me in the eye, "I don't care what your inner demons are telling you. You're a good person. You're the light of my life. I will never believe otherwise."

"You know … sometimes I've wondered what would happen if I lost you, Alex. Or worse, if I killed you myself. Because I went crazy. Because I somehow began to believe I was trapped in a conspiracy. If I ever hurt you, if I ever lost you because I gave in to my paranoia, I …"

"You won't."

"Maybe I am a prisoner. Maybe I am trapped and only by sacrificing you can I escape. Maybe I'll … I'll …"

"You won't."

"Aren't you afraid? Don't you think I'm a lunatic? A danger?"

"I'm not afraid of you, Jaina. And I don't think you're a lunatic."

"But I am … if I'm thinking these things … that means …"

"It means you're scared. It means you're afraid. You've seen the madness that can seize people, and it reminds you of your own fragility."

She smiled and kissed me. Slowly.

"But even if you think you're all alone in this world, I know you're not. Because I'm here. And whether you see me, or notice me, I'll always be here, protecting you."

"I … you're real, aren't you?"

"I am."

"You'll hold me, won't you?"

"I will."

"You … you won't think less of me, right? If I spout bullshit like this if I get scared? I don't want to push you away …"

"All I want is for you to be happy. And I'll do everything I can to help you."

Alex was smiling. She looked so warm, so loving.

"You are not my prisoner. You're my partner. My equal. My beloved."

We kissed.

"Whatever you're facing, whatever you're struggling with, I'll bear it with you. We'll go through everything together."

"I'm sorry, Alex. I'm so, so sorry."

"It's okay, Jaina. No matter what happens, everything's going to be okay. Trust me."

"Okay, I'll … try my best."

I could feel the softness of her chest. The warmth of her skin. The wetness of her lips as they kissed down my neck.

Yes, this was all real. It had to be.

"That's good enough for me, Jaina. Let's just take it one day at a time. Together."

"Yeah." I smiled. "Together forever."

Bliss

She was feeling me up from behind, as she kissed down my neck. I could feel the ticklishness on my nipples as she squeezed my breasts.

"I love you so much." She whispered as she kissed down my neck, her lips making my back feel all wet and ticklish.

"Hehehe." I giggled. "Keep going, Alex."

"Gladly," she whispered in my ear.

She tightened her grip on me in a backward embrace. I could feel her breasts press against my back.

"I'm so glad you're doing better now, Jaina."

"Really?" I muttered. "Alex, I know I've been giving you a hard time ..."

"Nonsense." She turned me around and looked me in the eye. "I know you've been through a lot, but right here, in the bedroom, I have nothing but the deepest love for you."

She kissed me on the lips, forcefully.

"I'm proud of you Jaina. I'm proud of the wonderful, amazing woman that you are. I want you to become stronger. I want you to assert yourself."

"I ... I can't be strong all the time," I murmured, as she continued to caress my body. "My doubts are always there, Alex, no matter what front I'm putting on. And I'm letting you see them because I trust you."

I buried my face into her chest.

"I trust you to be a safe harbor for me. I trust you to never use my weaknesses against me. No, it's more than trust. It's faith. I have faith in you, Alex."

I caressed her cheek as I felt my eyes wet with tears. "I just believe that you'll be by my side. Even if you hurt me, or let me down, I'll continue to have faith. I want to be with you no matter what. I love you so, so much!"

"Jaina ..." she held me gently, but firmly. "Thank you for believing in me so much."

My desires were guiding me to kiss her. Feel her. Savor her. And she was still whispering.

"In my arms, you will always be safe. My body will always accept you. My mind will always cherish you. My happy place is a place where I can bare it all for you."

She cupped my face into her hands, smiling with joy and reverence.

"Your love is the one thing I always look forward to, day after day. Keep these memories close to you, Jaina. Let them remind you how loved you are, how valued you are. And should fate, or even I disappoint you, remember the truth. This is the truth."

"Yeah." I smiled. "Yeah, this is the truth. Your love is the truth. Our love is the truth. I won't let anything get in the way of that. I know you'll always come back for me, Alex."

"Without a doubt," she whispered.

Our bodies were already in sync. Moving towards a sweet climax that would viscerally confirm our vows. A pleasure that would remain in our minds as another fond memory.

A memory of how much we meant to one another.

My Knight

"Mmm … so this is your new uniform," I whispered while feeling her up and kissing her.

"Yup. Custom-made. I had it designed with detachable plating. On the job, I'm hardened and ready for action. Off the job …" She smiled playfully. "I'm soft and flexible. Just for you."

"You can't be serious …" I giggled. "There's no way you'd redesign your armor just to spice up our sex life … would you?"

"I'm not joking, Jaina," she said, as I continued exploring her. "I wanted you to get the authentic Stellaris security experience. Whenever you want it, wherever you want it."

"You're a fucking cheater, Alex!" I tried to scold her but just ended up laughing instead. And despite the point I was trying to make, my actions were undercutting me.

I was turned on. Really, REALLY turned on.

"Is this your idea of payback?" I giggled as I continued to fondle her body. Yes, the uniform was form-fitting and skintight. And comfy to the touch.

"Indeed, it is. You gave me quite a time by becoming an activist lawyer, so now you get to enjoy me in the same uniform I wear when arresting your clients!"

She pushed against me until she was on top of me, her smile voracious and full of longing.

"Damn it, Alex, you're right! I am enjoying this. I'm enjoying this so, so much."

We were professional rivals these days, each working towards tipping the opposite ends of the scale. But together, we grounded each other. We balanced each other out.

And we never lost our love for each other. We never took things to heart. Somehow, our differences had only deepened our bonds instead of frayed them. I felt so, so fortunate to live such a life.

"I'm never going to see you the same way again when you're on duty, you know? I'll probably want to jump on you right there and then."

"Join the club. It takes a lot of effort for me to refrain from kissing you when I take Stellaris prisoners away from interrogation."

"Maybe we should do it anyway. Our relationship's no secret, Alex."

"Yeah, maybe," she said, while eagerly undressing me. As much as I'd felt her up, Alex's uniform was largely intact.

"But I want to keep our games in the bedroom, Jaina. Let's have all our fun where no one else can ruin the moment."

"You make a good point," I said, as I eagerly felt up her body again. Alex always had a great dressing sense but loving her in her uniform truly was an unforgettable experience. I didn't want to take it off so soon.

"I am sad you don't get paid that much though," she said, losing her playful tone and sounding rather somber. "You're still depending a lot on me and Stellaris. The other day, Becca was joking about how she could very easily use your vulnerabilities to crush you. And she's right. That doesn't seem fair to me."

"I don't care about that, Alex. Really." I smiled and continued to kiss her. "I know the score. You're stronger than me. You're more powerful. More dangerous. You could even have me jailed in connection with the bombing that nearly killed Becca. I know that you could easily ruin my prospects if you really wanted to. Heck, it's kind of become a kink of mine." I chuckled.

"And that's really … alright with you?"

"I believe in you, remember?" I smiled. "I trust you with my life, Alex. I have faith you'll protect me."

I finally began undressing her.

"You've told me not to fear you, and I don't. Quite the opposite. It's because I'm with you that I'm not afraid. It's because I'm with you that I feel free to live on my terms. And lastly …"

I caressed her cheek.

"I don't see you or Stellaris as my enemy at all. I'm just trying to provide some balance. Some accountability. I want to challenge you, Alex, but only because I want us to keep working together, in the interest of true justice."

"So, all this time, you've thought of me as a partner not just in love, but in the work we do?"

"Yeah, and I know that gets lost in the day-to-day nature of what we do. But that's the truth, Alex."

I kissed her down her exposed skin, relishing every moment.

"I have always, always wanted the best for you. In every sense."

"I'm sorry, Jaina. I … I didn't really think of it that way. I just assumed you were still acting out your apprehensions, that maybe we'd always be at odds in some way, but …"

She held me tightly as she kissed me.

"If you've always considered me an ally, I'll do everything in my power to live up to your faith in me. No one, whether they're within Stellaris or without, will ever harm a hair on your head."

"Alex …"

"I'm sorry. This was just supposed to be a fun little game, but I feel humbled, Jaina. I didn't realize that your love for me ran so deep, and it's my own fault for not reading between the lines. But your faith in me will be rewarded. I will be your knight, and your guardian, now and forever."

"I'm so happy to hear that, Alex." I smiled as I buried my face in her chest. "I'm so happy my beloved knight hasn't left me."

"She never will, Jaina," Alex whispered as we resumed loving each other, our excitement building up. "Her oath is unbreakable."

Pride

It was a cold night. The breeze was chilly. But I was comfortable. I was at peace.

Alex smiled as she continued to play with my hair and kissed me. I was lying on my back, using her body as my pillow while she leaned against a tree.

And we were just looking out, into the starry sky.

"I love you." She smiled and murmured. She looked so happy, being with me.

God, what did I ever do to deserve someone like her?

"So, I've heard this is quite the special month for people like us. The queer folk are out in full swing, celebrating how special they are. I'm pretty sure Stellaris got their mileage out of having a lesbian like you in their ranks."

"That they did, Jaina." She chuckled. "They did a special feature with me, and other queer employees for this month's magazine. I had to do a whole interview about my relationship with you."

She paused as she petted my hair, and kissed me once more,

"Of course, I'm going to pretend like it never happened. I wouldn't want to embarrass you with a corporate glorification of our love, after all."

"Oh really?" I said, a mischievous impulse rising within me, "And here I thought you considered Stellaris the saviors of this world, the chosen ones who'll guide us all to salvation!"

"Come on, Jaina," she said, chuckling.

"Alex, I'm just fooling around. I'll always stand with you, whatever it takes. I don't want to know about every dirty secret Stellaris or you are hiding. I don't want you to worry about protecting me from scandals, or whatever. I'll always believe in you, no matter what you're involved in."

"Jaina, you've ... you've been more gracious, more accepting of me than I could've ever asked for. I mean that." She caressed my cheek and gently kissed down my neck. "If I'd told my younger self ten years ago that I would meet someone like you, someone who'd always make me feel safe, and wanted, I wouldn't have believed her. I was honestly quite cynical of other people. Their motives, their agendas."

She looked me in the eye with an outright childlike expression. Like she was bringing all of her defenses down.

"But you ... you've been so genuine, right from the start. I may not have always agreed with you, and you might have given me a hard time over some things ... but I could always trust you. Always have faith in you. You have no idea how rare such a quality is, Jaina. You have no idea how special you are to me. Without you, I might have gone down a much darker path. A lonely path, where my own heart turned into ice. You saved me from that, Jaina."

"Alex, I ..."

I saved her? Me?

"And despite that, I was the one who betrayed you. I let you down during your time of need.

And even after that day, even after you forgave me, I kept projecting myself as the strong one, the powerful one. I … I needed you to think that I was the one protecting you. That you were the one who needed me. But I was always scared, Jaina. Scared of admitting how much I needed you. How much I relied on you. I've spent so long, believing that I needed to be strong…to rely only on my own strength."

Her actions were mirroring her words. Her grip on me was getting much tighter. She was clinging to me, crying on my shoulder. She sounded like she was begging me for something … like a scared child.

"But that's not true! I can't carry on alone, Jaina! I can't live without you! I need you, to keep me sane! To feel okay about things! If you're not around to accept me, to forgive me … I don't know if I could take it anymore!"

"A … Alex …" I had no words. Alex had always affirmed me. Always valued me. But to pour her heart out to me with such intensity. Such desperation … it was hard to know what to say.

"Just let me hold you, please. Just let me stay with you. Don't leave me out in the cold, Jaina. I … I don't ever want to be alone again!"

"You're not alone," I murmured. "I love you, Alex. I want to stay with you. I want to be with you."

I looked her in the eye. "And I never, ever want you to be unhappy. I never want to see you broken, or sad. You're really, really important to me."

"Oh, Jaina ..." she was still sobbing as she held me close as if I might slip away at any moment.

Even though I knew I wasn't going anywhere. Even though I knew I'd always stay with her.

Especially if this was how much she leaned on me.

"You've always been so grounded, Jaina. So humble. With you, I can appreciate the small things. The simple things. It's only because of you that I can remember what truly matters in my life. The places I've been, the things I've done ..."

She looked at her hands in horror. In shame. Almost as though she was feeling disgusted with herself.

"I can only live with them because I know that I can live differently with you. I can be different with you. There's more to life than the ugliness I've seen. Ugliness I've ... perpetuated. There is beauty, there is innocence, there is hope. Because despite everything, I still managed to have a life with you."

I held her close.

"You're right, Alex. You don't have to define yourself by your worst experiences, or by your darkest deeds. I don't care what you've done, because I know you love me. I don't care how much you hate yourself, because I know you're lovable. I don't care what anyone says about you, because I will never give up on you! You're the one I love, now and forever, and nothing will ever change that."

"Yes ... you're my sanctuary ... you're my haven, Jaina."

"I'll be whoever you need me to be, Alex." I kissed her. Slowly. Deeply. "I'll be the light that guides you, whenever you're in doubt, whenever you're in despair. Because you deserve a happy life. You deserve a hopeful life. I know that to be true, Alex."

"I love you so, so much Jaina. I'm so glad I fell in love with you. So, so glad."

"So am I, Alex. No matter when or where you doubt my love for you, I will prove it, over and over again. I will always fight for you."

As I heard the crackling of fireworks, I turned around to look at the sky. Yes, they were sparkling with celebration. People celebrating their unique identities, their love, their pride.

And though I knew it wasn't true, I wanted to pretend that the fireworks lighting the sky were there just for us. As if fate itself had affirmed our love for each other.

"Happy Pride Month, babe," I said to Alex, as we went for another kiss.

Roots

"Have I loosened you up enough?" Alex whispered as she caressed my body. I felt so warm, so happy. But also, a little greedy.

"No," I replied. "More."

She chuckled and resumed pleasing me, exciting and pampering my body like a skilled practitioner. Since she knew me better than anyone, she was not only pushing all the right buttons but pushing them in the right order, the right intensity. It felt so comfortable. So … familiar.

"My baby, my precious baby," she murmured. "I'll always love you so much, my lovely baby."

"Mmm, yes. I know you will, Alex. With you, I'm just … happy."

A warm pleasure soon pulsed through me, and I arched my body as I received it. "Yes!" I whispered. "Yes! Thank you, Alex! Thank you so much!"

She kissed me on the lips, deeply and forcefully.

"I love you, Jaina. My precious, precious Jaina."

We wrapped our arms around each other as I sank my head into her chest, enveloped in her warmth. Her protection.

It felt really familiar now. Like a comforting memory I could go back to, whenever I fell into doubt or dread. Her body. Her warmth. Her yearning, and her love, for me.

It had softened up each and every day of mine. I was so blessed to have someone for whom I could always let my guard down.

I could feel the gentle rhythm of her hand, as it began caressing my hair. The wetness of her lips, as they kissed yet another part of my body. She was still hungry. Still satiating herself.

"Don't stop," I whispered. And so she didn't.

"I'm sorry I was away for so long," she murmured. "I know you've had to spend a lot of days without me, so I wanted our time to be special when I came back. And I wanted to put you first tonight."

"You've been really good to me, Alex." I was still smiling. "And I suppose some level of absence does remind us how much we love each other. How much we want each other."

"It does. God, I've missed you so much," she said, hungrily asking my body for more, even as I was reciprocating.

Her aggression ultimately turned to satisfaction, as she wrapped her arms around me, her voice teeming with joy. "Ah! That was so good! So, so good!"

I pet her hair and kissed her, over and over again.

"I'll always do my best for you, Alex. I want you to be happy whenever you're with me."

"Jaina, you're enough, just as you are." She smiled and cupped my face in her hands. "I was always thinking of you, thinking of how I'd be safe again when we got back together. And that's how I feel right now. This is my haven. You are my haven."

"You're ... really leaning on me these days. It's going to take some getting used to," I murmured.

"I understand," she said, as we held each other closely, her warmth engulfing me. "And I'm grateful, Jaina. To know I can let my guard down around you means so much to me."

"I'm really happy to hear that. You're such a fascinating person, you know. There's so much I'm constantly learning about you. I'm glad I was worthy of being so close to you."

She giggled.

"I'm an open book for you, Jaina. If you want to know anything more about me, all you have to do is ask."

"Okay," I said, kissing her neck as I fondled her breasts. "Tell me where you came from, Alex. I want to know what made you into the woman you are today."

"Alright. It's going to be a long story though," she said playfully. "And I don't want you nodding off."

"And here I was getting so comfortable." I kissed her on the lips and took my time to savor it. "Okay, deal. I'll listen to everything."

"Alright, well, I've mentioned my Vander lineage before, right?"

"Mmm, you have."

"Well, you wouldn't be surprised to hear this, but the knights of Vander were originally quite male-dominated. My family was quite traditionalist about gender roles, among other things. A woman, and especially a lesbian like me, probably wouldn't have been acknowledged as a legitimate heir if things hadn't changed very, very recently."

"Oh, Alex," I said as I caressed her face. "I'm sorry to hear that."

"Of course, social movements radically changed the environment around our family, so we had to make some adjustments to adapt. The Vanders couldn't exactly get away with disowning their queer children after a certain point, you know. But there was still that conservative power dynamic. The preferential treatment given to so-called normal men and women who'd be good-old-fashioned warriors and mothers respectively. Someone like me, who couldn't fit those traditional roles, was still kind of an outcast."

"I didn't know you had it so tough, Alex."

"No, it's not like that," Alex chuckled. "What I'm trying to say is, I had it better than a lot of my forebears. I was one of the lucky ones. I never wanted for anything. I was never an outcast. And it was all thanks to my grandmother."

"Your grandmother?"

"Yeah. It was during her time that the Vanders first allied with Stellaris. Back then, a massive political upheaval was taking place. Stellaris had raised its own private army to neutralize the threat of the national military that sought to push back against their dominance, and my great-grandfather was among the generals. He lost his life in the ensuing civil war, and Stellaris's forces were routed. My grandfather also died due to an untimely illness, so only my grandmother could take over. And she changed everything, Jaina."

"Wait, hold up. Stellaris turned against our own national military?!"

"Oh. Oh yeah, that's not information the public is privy to, are they?" Alex chuckled. "The arms dealers and private military contractors had a massive falling out with the federal government and defected to Stellaris to better protect their interests. Stellaris wanted to completely privatize the military, something the government was opposed to. So there was a war."

"And your grandmother fought in it."

"She did more than that." Alex smiled proudly and kissed me. "She turned the tide. Her fresh approach, her unorthodox methods were what finally brought about the dawn of a new era. We negotiated a ceasefire wherein the government's capabilities were severely curtailed, allowing private armies to dominate the military. Some defense contractors broke away from Stellaris to establish their own business. Many others were absorbed into Stellaris, making us by far the most dominant military force to this day."

"I … I had no idea …"

"I'm really sorry for not telling you sooner Jaina." She kissed me. "My family brought me up to be careful about what I told others, but you're the love of my life. I should've opened up to you a long time ago."

She looked so happy. So proud. There was a childlike joy in the way she was recounting her family's history, even though my own feelings were considerably more … mixed.

I didn't want to burden Alex with my conflicting emotions, however, so I put on a smile and said, "You sound really proud of her, Alex. Was she good to you?"

"She was. She loved me unconditionally, Jaina. When I came out to her, she was actually happy for me. She used her position as head of the Vander household to completely dismantle the entrenched traditions and prejudices of old.

And I wanted to be by her side as she did that. I wanted to make my grandmother proud."

"Is that why you joined Stellaris? Is that why you believe in them so much?"

"Yes. But I was also doing it for myself. I wanted to carve my own path as a Vander. To become a knight who could be a woman, who could be queer. My grandmother had broken the mold, and I wanted to craft a new mold. I wanted to redefine what could be possible in the Vander household. And to do that, I knew I had to be strong. To be powerful. To be at the forefront of changing the world, just as my grandmother had. And the people at Stellaris are the only ones who can do it, Jaina. Only they can evolve humanity ... this world ... in the right direction."

"Your grandma worked with Stellaris to take control of this country, and now you want to carry on her legacy. By working with Stellaris to take control of the entire world."

She smiled joyfully as she kissed me deeply and held me close.

"Yes! That's my life's mission! My ultimate goal! I'm so glad you finally understand, Jaina!"

"Yes." I continued to smile, but I could feel the tears clouding my eyes. "I do understand, Alex."

"Hey." She was wiping away my tears. "What's wrong, Jaina?"

"Nothing ..." I murmured. "Nothing's wrong. It's just, to look so deeply into the heart of another person ... I think I'm just overwhelmed."

"Aw, it's okay." She hugged me. Kissed me. Did her best to comfort me. "You can cry on my shoulder whenever you want, Jaina."

"It all makes sense now, you know," I said. "Everything you've done, everything you've said. Everything about you has fallen into place for me."

I caressed her body. I was fighting so desperately to curtail the anxiety that was overwhelming me, *begging* me not to say anymore.

"Everything, except one thing. Why do you love me?"

"Huh?" She pulled back, looking genuinely confused by my question.

"Alex ... I've been critical of Stellaris from the beginning. I never thought they were a force for good, I kept speaking out against them, I even actively got in their way as a Lightwarden, and as an attorney. I've been ... an obstacle to your goals. So why am I still with you?"

"Jaina …" She leaned in and kissed me. "You're wrong. You're not an obstacle. You've never been an obstacle. You just have a mind of your own, that's different from mine. All that makes you is human."

"But this … this is everything to you, so …"

"No. No, it isn't. I realized that when I saw you with the Lightwardens in the warzone I'd created. When I saw you in the interrogation room as you broke down. I knew then that I didn't care if you were on Stellaris's side. My only concern was if you could still care about me. I cannot accept a world in which I lose you, Jaina."

"But why? This goes completely against …"

"No, it doesn't!" She raised her voice. "Ever since that day, haven't we done our best to stand by each other? To respect each other? You accepted me, and what I was doing. Even if you had your reservations about Stellaris, you didn't set out to destroy them. Even when you became an attorney and began fighting us again, we were still growing. Still flourishing. Stellaris will change the world. You haven't stopped that at all."

She kissed me again.

"And more than that, making you happy, showing my love for you … it fulfils me in ways that my original mission never could. Because you have disagreements, because you're vulnerable, I know that you're real, Jaina. I know that I am nurturing and protecting a real human being, who I can come home to day after day. Bringing about a new future would feel so empty if I didn't have someone to share it with, if I couldn't show someone the wonders that await us! I'm happy that you're around to challenge me, Jaina! Because once I share the fruits of our efforts with you, once you can bask in the glory Stellaris will bring, I know I'll have earned my victory! You'll be by my side, to witness the dawn of a new world, and I'll personally make sure we experience its beauty, together!"

"And what if I don't agree? What if I don't like the world you and Stellaris bring about?"

"That … that would be painful, true. But it's pain I'm willing to bear. I know you have many issues with the methods we've used. I know about your misgivings about what we've had to, what we'll need to sacrifice for the future we're building. But all this is to make people happy. And I need to see that happiness for myself, reflected in the eyes of someone who knows me better than anyone else. I need to see your happiness, Jaina. As long as I have that, it will be enough."

"I was happy tonight, Alex. And I've been happy for a long time, just because you were there with me. Loving me, comforting me. I've shared my happiness with you for so long, isn't that enough? You don't need to do any more. You don't need to sacrifice anymore."

"Jaina, everything's already falling into place. It's only a matter of time before Stellaris's dreams, and my dreams, are realized. Why are you so afraid? Don't you trust me?"

"Alex, I know your work's … been hurting you. The way your actions haunt you. The guilt you feel. You've opened up to me about all this. I … I just don't want to lose the Alex I love."

"Jaina … it's true. The hard choices I've had to make, the people I've cast aside for the greater good, it all seems utterly hideous in the moment. That's why it haunts me. And that's why I looked to you for comfort. Because I knew you hadn't been hardened by the harsh path I had to walk. Because I knew I could protect you from ever having to face such horrors yourself. I've paid a heavy price for fulfilling my mission, but I paid it willingly. Even if my actions and

Stellaris's actions haunt me, I wouldn't change a thing. Because I need to be the change. I need to shape the best possible future for all who are worthy."

She kissed me deeply and held me close.

"I know I'll always have your love, and I'm grateful for that. I know you just want to protect me, to help me. But I don't want you to worry. I will never leave you. And I can't lose myself, because I'm not conflicted about what I want. I'm not at war with myself. So, rest easy, okay?"

What she said was the undeniable truth. I knew that now. Who was I kidding? Someone as driven as her, as strong as her, couldn't possibly be a victim.

I'd only ever seen her softer side because she loved me, but I always knew, deep down, that she was no different from the conquerors, the expansionists and the imperialists I'd read about in the history books. Stellaris was in the midst of a global mission to subjugate and civilize all corners of the globe, and my beloved Alex would see their mission done willingly and relentlessly.

That was why all my efforts to oppose Stellaris as a Lightwarden, as a lawyer, only lead to small victories. Victories rendered utterly inconsequential in the grand scheme of things, as Stellaris continued its march for dominance. The simple truth was, Alex was determined to win, and I didn't want her to lose.

Even if I expressed my disapproval, even if I spoke of my misgivings, I could never let Alex believe that what she set out to do was wrong. I could never let her believe that Stellaris was a force of evil. I couldn't allow myself, or anyone, to desecrate the very identity she'd built around herself. As the successor to her grandmother's will. As the brave visionary who would carry forward the Vander legacy by changing the entire world.

As the woman who loved her, I had only one goal. To ensure her happiness, no matter what. Just as she would spare no expense to ensure my happiness in the new world she was building.

"Alex …" I kissed her neck and buried my face in her bosom. "When your mission is over, I'd be happy to see your new world with my own eyes."

"Jaina." She smiled tenderly and kissed me. "Of course, you will. And remember, what's mine is yours. We will live our wonderful new lives together."

"And one more thing ..." I caressed her face, looking at her with nothing but the deepest love in my heart. "Please don't forget the wonders we already have right here. I want to spend as much time as I can with you, Alex. I want to be next to you. Talking to you, feeling your touch and making love to you means so, so much to me."

"I'm sorry I had to be away for a while, Jaina. But you don't need to worry anymore. The hardest work is behind us now. I feel ... really carefree, you know?"

"Then I'm going to make full use of you." I giggled as I playfully fondled her body. The body that had been my biggest source of warmth and comfort ever since I fell in love.

Alex pushed back until she was on top of me, aggressively kissing all over my body. "You still have a lot of energy left in you, huh?"

"I guess peering into your heart was quite a stimulating experience, Alex. I feel like a new woman already!"

"Yeah, I feel pretty energized too. We've really shared a lot of ourselves with each other, haven't we?"

"As we should," I said as I cupped her face and kissed her as deeply as I could. "We love each other, don't we?"

"Yeah." She wrapped her arms around me. "Yeah, we do. We belong together, Jaina. Forever and always."

"I will always stand by you and do everything I can for you, Alex," I said, allowing myself to get lost within her. "No matter what."

"My precious, precious baby." I heard her whisper, as my body guided me to our next climax. "You're everything to me."

Our Universe

"So, you did it again. You got us another home."

"Yes, a generous reward from Stellaris for my services," Alex said, as she gleefully took me by the hand and showed me around. "I find it quite fitting you know, having three homes for us."

"What do you mean?"

"All will be explained, in time," she said in a playfully cryptic tone.

This house was by far the largest and most lavish one I'd seen, and that was saying something. There were so many rooms that just seemed like placeholders, like their true purpose was yet to be realized.

And then there were our rooms.

A beautiful bedroom with a big, soft bed. We fooled around quite a bit there, as Alex and I rolled around, kissed each other and felt each other, but stopped short of taking off our clothes.

An entertainment lounge that was smaller than I expected it to be. It seemed clear that Alex wanted this to be an intimate setting, where the two of us could watch a movie or play a game without feeling too overwhelmed.

And a dining room and kitchen that already seemed stocked with gourmet meal kits that had me very intrigued. Dinner was going to be a fascinating affair indeed.

"So, how is it?" Alex said as we finished our tour.

"It's ... it's amazing. What we have here, goes beyond my wildest dreams." I smiled and kissed her. "You're really making me feel like a princess."

"You know I'd never pass up an opportunity to do that." Alex chuckled. "You deserve nothing less."

"I love you so much, Alex. So, so much," I said as I wrapped her arms around her and pulled her close.

I always felt so warm, so comforted and so safe in her arms. And this home was giving me a similar feeling. I knew that here I would want for nothing. Here, I would always belong.

"It's all fallen into place," Alex said. "I've accomplished everything I set out to do, but I've been blessed with so much more than what my mission could've given me. I've been blessed with you, Jaina."

"What are you saying, Alex? Is your mission … over?"

"My original one, yes. Why do you think Stellaris gave me this home? Because we've established our dominance across every corner of the globe, and now we get to shape the world to our design. Everyone who led the efforts has been generously rewarded."

"This is what you wanted all along, isn't it? This is why you climbed the ranks, why you remained loyal to Stellaris every step of the way."

I looked her in the eye.

"I'm really happy for you, Alex. I'm so glad your dreams came true."

"And now, I can focus on a new dream, Jaina. I can focus on being with you."

"Huh? What do you mean?"

"You know why I'm so happy we have three homes? Because now we can mark each stage of our lives, Jaina. We already had a home for our early lives, when we'd just fallen in love, gotten to know each other, seen each other grow, and accepted each other. And for our later lives, when we've reached the end of our rope, and are spending our twilight years side by side. And now, we have a place, for our middle lives."

"Middle lives?"

"By next year, Jaina, I'll be retiring as Stellaris's Chief of Security. I'll take up a new position on their Advisory Board. There, I will be advising and deliberating with other board members on what direction Stellaris should take on the new world project, but I won't be involved in any heavy responsibilities. You know what that means?"

"Um ..."

Before I could say anymore, she cut me off with a fierce kiss.

"That means I'll be spending most of my time with you, Jaina! You'll become my primary focus! Every single day, I want to make new memories with you, I want to build something new with you!"

"You want to shift your focus away from Stellaris … for me?"

"Yes! That's the new chapter I want to start, Jaina! And I want to start it in this home, for our middle lives."

"I see," I murmured, "So that's how it is. Your ambitions have been realized, and you want to decide what to do next with me."

"Oh, Jaina." Alex smiled and kissed me again. "What we do next doesn't have to be one big thing. We can do lots of things, little by little. Honestly, I don't even care if I spend the next two years just lazing around, adoring you and making love to you. There's no need to rush in starting a family."

"Family?!"

"Oh, it slipped out huh?" Alex chuckled. "Well, okay. Yes, starting a family with you was what I had in mind for the long-term, Jaina. But I was hoping not to put any pressure on you this early."

"You … you want to have children … with me?"

"Yes, with you, and with no one else," Alex said softly, as we shared another kiss. "I do not doubt that you'll be an amazing mother to them. You're the only person I ever want to start a family with, Jaina. Which is why we'll only to this if you're ready."

"You … you really thought this far ahead, Alex? I had no idea …"

"I know this is a lot to take in, Jaina." Alex smiled as she gently cupped my face. "Which is why I want you to take your time. Let's just enjoy our time together, day by day, until you're ready for the next step. And even if you never are." She leaned in and kissed me. "I will still spend the rest of my life with you. We're already a family, just as we are, and if you want it to stay that way, I don't mind."

"B-but is that really okay with you? I mean, you're carrying the Vander bloodline, and …"

"And I'm not beholden to it. I told you, didn't I? I wanted to redefine the Vanders. I led them as a woman. As a lesbian. And, as a lesbian, I will only carry the bloodline forward with the consent of the woman I love. Sticking to my principles is the best way for me to define my family's legacy. I will not be swayed by the trappings of conventional wisdom."

"You … you really trust me that much? You … really want to leave it all … to me?"

"Of course I do. You're the love of my life, after all."

"O-okay. As long as I'm not burdening you, Alex ..."

"No." She cut me off with a kiss. "You've never been a burden. Far from it. It's because of you that I can still feel complete. It's because of you that I know that my dream to change the world meant something. Because you're going to live in this new world with me. And if we ever bring new life into this world, they too will live in this beautiful world we've made for them."

"We made this world? I don't know, I only got in your way ..."

"No." She cut me off again as she kissed me. "You've been my ally every step of the way. Never my enemy. You said it yourself, remember? Even when you challenged me, you still wanted me to succeed. You still believed in me. So, I owe my success to you, Jaina. I owe it to you more than anyone else because no one knows me as you do. No one understands me like you do."

"A-Alex, I ... I love you!" I said as I burst into tears. "Oh God, I love you so much! So, so much! I ... I don't ... I don't deserve everything you've given me! You're ... you're too kind to me! This is too much!"

"Shh ..." She sounded completely unfazed. "It's okay, Jaina. It's all okay. Everything's going to be okay."

Her hands were comforting me. Caressing my hair. Rubbing my back. Wiping my tears.

"I heard somewhere that when two people truly love each other, they can create a whole universe together. A universe that belongs just to them. And its potential is infinite. It can become anything they want it to be, so long as they build it together."

She looked me in the eye.

"Let's build our own universe together, Jaina. Something that will grow, and change, but will always be ours and ours alone. Let's put our all into it. And we'll work on it for the rest of our lives."

"Our ... our universe. Yes, that sounds beautiful, Alex."

"I'm so happy to hear you say that, Jaina. So, let's make more memories together."

We kissed each other.

"Let's show our love for each other."

We felt each other.

"Let's feel every emotion. Positive, negative. Affirming, conflicting. And no matter what we feel, no matter what we say, we'll be safe. Because it's our universe, and ours alone."

I could feel the warmth and softness of the bed.

"No one else can understand our love. No one else can ever get between us. We accept each other. We support each other. And we will always protect each other."

My skin was bare, and so was hers.

"And whatever we create will be beautiful. Because we did it together. Because we can do anything together."

Yes. I relished her. I longed for her. I hungered for her. And she was right here, ready to satisfy me.

"Yes! I love you! I love you, Alex Vander!"

"And I love you too, Jaina Marshall!"

A Princess of the Stars

It was a truly liberating feeling, to trust in my beloved so completely. When she smiled, I smiled. When she was joyful, so was I. No longer did my conscience question the world she'd built around me. No longer did I feel compelled to deny my happiness out of sorrow for those who suffered.

I knew that I would never leave Alex's side, and that was all the reason I needed to be happy.

"And this will be your planet." Alex drew another circle on our scrapbook, followed by making it orbit around the galactic sun.

When she'd spoken of building our universe together, I knew she meant it metaphorically, alluding to the way two lovers can create new life, or the transformative potential of long-term romantic intimacy. But I wanted to take things a step further. I really did want to create a universe in our imagination. It would belong to just the two of us, as we lost ourselves in our fantasies, completely unconcerned about anything else.

"But why don't you create one of your own?"

"Because knights are sworn to serve, not rule," Alex said. "I am happy to live a life of service. But you, Jaina, deserve more."

She leaned in and kissed me as she gently fondled my body.

"You deserve a planet to call your own. Right now, you're still a fledgling princess, but soon you'll grow into a queen. A queen with a commanding will that'll enrapture everyone around you! And until that day comes …"

"Let me guess." I cut her off with a kiss. "You'll protect me, care for me, and love me with all your heart?"

"Without question." Alex pulled me close and kissed me hungrily, aggressively. I knew then that our storytelling time was over and put the scrapbook away.

"I wonder if it's proper for a princess to court her own servants." I giggled.

"I will bear whatever punishment it takes, so long as I have your heart."

"Well …" I fondled her breasts and smiled with intense longing. "You do have it, my knight."

And so, we lost ourselves in each other, our bodies so familiar, and yet so appetizing to one another.

These were such wonderful, carefree days. I truly did have Alex almost all to myself, and she made it worth my while, day after day. Loving her, talking to her, decoding her heart. All of it filled my days with an unending fullness as if exploring her was all I needed to feel like my life had meaning.

We were constantly challenging each other and creating new worlds with each other. Even when I couldn't quite put my finger on it, I knew that my mind was being transformed and enriched whenever I opened up to Alex, and I suspected it was the same for her. I believed the key was the gratitude we had for finding each other. Our differences, which earlier bred conflict and tension, now empowered our moments together, gave us more to discuss, more to explore, more to change.

Neither of us had our guard up anymore as we opened our hearts to each other. Yes, getting close to others could be painful. It could be difficult. But now that we had overcome so many of the barriers that had chafed us, we felt nothing but sweetness, warmth and comfort around each other.

As part of my pampering, Alex would often take me to these high-class parties that the aces and top dogs in Stellaris attended. And I no longer looked upon them with apprehension or contempt. Because they were Alex's friends, her comrades, the people who gave her life meaning. No matter what I thought of their actions, I could never rob my beloved of those who were so foundational to her happiness.

And so, if she wanted to pamper me, I'd let her. If she wanted me to enjoy the finest cuisine, the finest fashions and the finest music, I would. I would embrace her affection for me wholeheartedly. I would become the princess she always saw me as.

"Come on," she said as she took my hand.

I simply smiled and let her take me wherever she wanted to.

Because she loved me, so did the world. Everywhere I went, people were glad to see me, glad to serve me, and there was no end to the fun I could have. I knew that all the favors I was receiving were simply a way to reward Alex for what she'd done, but I wanted to reward her too. And I believed her when she said that my smile was the greatest reward she could hope for, and so I smiled for her, and I would keep smiling for her.

"Ah!" She moaned as we made love in a resort Alex had specially booked for us on this trip. A nice, lovely nature reserve that served as an amazing vacation spot. And since Alex had so much free time these days, we could come over here again and again.

"Yes!" I whispered, as my body spasmed with pleasure. "You're so wonderful, Alex! You're amazing!"

"Jaina ..." She smiled as she caressed my cheek and kissed me again. "I'm so glad you're enjoying yourself. It means so much to me."

"I know." I smiled. "I want to make the most of our time, Alex. I want to enjoy every single day I spend with you."

I wrapped my arms around her and pulled her towards me and began to kiss her and fondle her to my heart's content.

"I'm really, really grateful for everything you've done for me, and I want to show it. I love the world you've built around me."

"Oh, Jaina …" She paused for a moment. "I … I know that Stellaris has done a lot that …"

I cut her off with a kiss. "I'm not talking about Stellaris. I'm talking about you. Everything you've done for me, everything you've shown me, was for my happiness, right? Well, I accept your gifts. I'm celebrating what you've done Alex. Nothing else."

Yes. If there was one person I would never turn against, one person I would unwaveringly protect no matter what anyone said, it was Alex. And so, I would always be grateful for all the happiness she'd brought me.

But that was as far as my unconditional devotion went. My only wish now was to protect my future with her, no matter who or what got in our way.

"Okay." She smiled. "I get it now. I am enough for you. I'm all you need."

Alex kissed and fondled me.

"I will protect you and cherish you, Jaina. For the rest of my days."

"That's all I needed to hear." I smiled as I basked in her warmth. "Nothing else matters, Alex."

"Yeah. Nothing else matters."

Even though we did have just three houses to our name, I was getting the sense that in practice, the number of places where we could live was a whole lot more. The rooms we booked during hotel visits, and resort visits, as well as an assortment of high-end rented flats were ours in all but name. We paid nominal rates for living in all the places we didn't technically own, and somehow no one else ever happened to be using them.

This must've been a hidden perk Alex was rewarded thanks to her exemplary work for Stellaris. She must've felt so happy that she could make full use of the benefits provided to her, for my sake. If I hadn't been with her, all these places we went to, all the wonders she showed me would've felt rather lonely. I could tell that her circle of friends had grown somewhat turbulent as of late. With the people at Stellaris so preoccupied with protecting their status, many would've seen Alex as a threat, given how she'd surpassed most of them.

My love for her had nothing to do with any of that. I was by her side since she was a trainee, and I would've remained by her side regardless of how her relationship with Stellaris changed. And she knew that.

I loved her, and only her.

"This is a pretty secluded place," I said, as we walked along the footpath the following day, marveling at the greenery around us.

"It is." Alex smiled. "This area was never open to the public, after all. I was able to pull a few strings to allow ourselves to visit after Stellaris annexed this island. But we're never fully opening this place up. Tourists would only pollute it."

"Yeah, I wouldn't want this place to become a littering ground. I want it to stay just the way it is."

"So do I." Alex kissed me. "And Stellaris has no interest in mining this place for resources either. We'll all protect this nice little corner, where nature can thrive."

"Alex ..." I kept kissing her, over and over. "You've really made sure I never get bored, haven't you?"

"Yeah," she said and smiled. "I want you to enjoy this new world. I want you to be happy."

"You're with me, Alex." I held her close as we kept kissing. "Of course, I'll be happy."

"Jaina ..." Alex eventually pulled back and pointed towards the skies. "See those birds?"

"Yeah?"

"You know, no matter what the state of the world is, they always take flight when they want to. They might run into an accident, they might be captured or killed by hunters, or they might lose their way. But no matter what, they choose to fly."

"They're creatures of instinct, aren't they? The concerns of the world don't hold them back. They don't think themselves out of what they want to do."

"No, they don't." She smiled wistfully as we kissed again. "I ... I suppose in a way I've also been flying all over, Jaina. I relentlessly pursued my lifelong mission, regardless of anyone's doubts. Regardless ... of even your doubts."

"Alex ..." I gently brushed her hair, but she simply smiled at me, as if telling me not to worry.

"I want to ... I need to believe that what I did was for the best. But I know that not everyone feels that way. But even as I knew that I'd be opposed, that I'd even be hated, I spread my wings and I flew, regardless of where I would end up. Because I wanted to do this."

I smiled as I pet her hair, gently nudging her to go on.

"And ever since I met you, I dreamed of the day when I'd show you how wonderful things could be. I wanted to prove myself to you. I wanted to show you that my dreams could make you happy. And they did! I'm so glad you're happy, Jaina!"

She pulled me in close and held me tightly as she brushed my hair with her palms, fondled my chest, and kissed down my neck.

It felt good. It all felt so good.

"You're the love of my life, Alex. If you're happy, I'm happy."

"I know, Jaina. I know. But ..."

She pulled back, and she was still smiling, but her eyes looked a little sadder.

"I know how much I've made you give up as I pursued my goals. I know how much you held back from following your convictions because of me. You've tried so hard to not get in my way. You even forgave me when I hurt you. I'm just ... sorry you couldn't be as free as I was."

"Alex …" I leaned in and kissed her, deeply. "I … I don't know if I'd have it in me to change the world. I'm not a visionary like you. Sure, I didn't agree with a lot of what you did, what you believed, but …"

I could feel a lump form in my throat, as I tried to hold back from bursting into tears again.

"But nothing would be worth the price of losing you, Alex! Nothing! I'd never ever forsake the love that was right in front of me! I don't care about high-minded abstractions like the greater good if it means giving up on the happiness I have with you! A world where I have your love is good enough for me, I don't care what else becomes of it!"

"I see." Relief washed over her face as she kissed me again. "Then you can leave it all to me, Jaina. I'll make sure that this world is worthy of you. I'll make sure that no matter what happens, my love will always reach you. You can relax and enjoy yourself as much as you want. I'll take care of everything else."

"Alex … please stay with me. That's all I want."

"Of course, Jaina." We kissed again. "I promised you, didn't I? I'm shifting my focus to you. To my life with you. And I'll be more than happy if the rest of our days went by just like this."

"Okay." I smiled. "I … I just thought that you might try to go off again, on some grand mission for me …"

"I won't. I'm not going anywhere. We'll stay together, Jaina."

"That's good. I love you, Alex. Please don't ever leave my side."

In response, she simply smiled and whispered, "You have my word, princess."

I caressed her cheek as I whispered back, "It's almost nighttime, isn't it? Dinner will be ready soon, and then …" I kissed her fiercely. "I want you for as long as it takes."

Precious

"Welcome home!" I said, and immediately rushed over to her and wrapped her in a tight embrace.

"Jaina!" She yelped in shock, but I didn't relent. Instead, I peppered her with as many kisses as I could.

"Wow, someone's in a good mood today," she chuckled.

"Well, I just really want you right now." I leaned in and kissed her more slowly. Deeply. "I know we're pretty used to each other most of the time, but today that won't be enough. I'm going to squeeze you for everything you have!"

I tightened my hold on her, just to illustrate my point.

"Oh, Jaina ..." Alex was smiling warmly, clearly floored by my show of affection. "Thank you."

We kept kissing as Alex slowly made her way back into the house.

"You know, you have pretty sharp instincts," Alex murmured. "Just when I'm starting to get bored, or worn out from the daily grind, there you are to comfort me."

"I just like making you happy, Alex. I want to do my best for you." We kissed again. "Our life is a sea of moments, many of which just pass us by before we know it. I just want to make sure you have something worth remembering from time to time."

"I'll do my best to remember how you're being today, Jaina. For you to be so happy around me ... that means a lot."

We settled down on a nearby couch and just held each other close as we savored each other's bodies. I was longing for her so much, but that was even more reason not to rush this. I wanted to appreciate her as much as I possibly could.

"So, how'd the meeting go?" I whispered as she kissed my neck.

"It was fine. I came up with some more recommendations on how to strengthen the security of our holdings. Kind of ironic that I retired from my Chief of Security position and yet that's the area where they constantly seek my advice."

"You must've been really good at your job then." I smiled and felt her breasts from over her sweater. "I think it's quite an accomplishment for them to still value your input."

"I'm glad you're happy for me." She chuckled. "In fact, hearing you praise me just made me feel a whole lot better about my day."

"Oh?" I smiled playfully. "Are the higher-ups being stingy with their kind words, Alex?"

"No, that's not it, it's just ..." She abruptly leaned in and kissed me fiercely. "Seeing you happy feels a bit more ... meaningful? I mean you are the person that matters the most to me, so if I'm doing right by you that just makes me feel like I'm doing okay. That I'll be okay."

"Hey." I kissed her back. "You know you don't have to work so hard for me, right Alex? I want to be here to comfort you, to make you happier. You don't have to earn any of that."

"That's not what I mean, Jaina." Alex smiled tenderly. "I want to work hard for you. I promised you, remember? That I'd make a world worthy of you."

She pressed against me as her hands went under my shirt, and I could feel them exploring my skin, my abdomen, my breasts.

"I know that a stable life, a pleasant life is what you need the most, which is why I changed my schedule to prioritize you. Why I vowed to spend most of my time with you."

She leaned in and we kissed.

"But your words have always stuck with me, Jaina. There are so many things I could've done better. We all could've done better. And we put our blinders on and sacrificed so much in the name of our ambition, despite your protests. I know that the world we live in today is a far cry from the way you would've envisioned it, Jaina."

"Alex, come on. You made that choice, didn't you? And I stood by you, because I wanted you to be happy, because I wanted your dreams to come true. If you're telling me that all of that was for …"

"No, no, please don't misunderstand. I … I guess I'm not explaining myself very well," she chuckled. "Everything I did to bring forth Stellaris's vision for our future, I would do so again. I had to fulfil my mission. I had to realize my dream. Looking back on it, I know I wouldn't have stopped. And it means everything to me that you stayed with me despite all of that. I will always, always be grateful that you accepted the future that I was fighting for, Jaina."

"Alex." I smiled and caressed her cheek. "I accepted everything because I love you. Because I believe in you. I just want you to be happy with the path you've chosen. Nothing else."

"Jaina, what I'm trying to say is that … that I never forgot about your dreams. I just couldn't support them very well because they seemed too intractable with what Stellaris was seeking. I kept acting like your ideals would just get in the way, and so I ultimately cast them aside."

She kissed me again. Slowly. Deeply.

"And because you love me, you forgave me for it. As long as I was happy, it didn't matter to you that my ambitions had superseded yours. But all of that is behind me, Jaina. I chased my dreams and reached the summit by casting aside everything that was in my way. Corporate rule, Stellaris rule is so entrenched across the globe it would take a monumental revolution to undo it. And I was one of the people who made that happen."

"What are you trying to tell me, Alex?"

"Jaina, I …" She kissed me and tightened her hold on me. "Goddamit I love you so much. It's amazing how well you've put up with me, how devoted you are to understanding me. Where would I be without you?"

"Well, you're not without me, are you?" I giggled.

"No, and I'm so glad I'm not."

She wrapped her arms around me and laid her head on my shoulder. Her voice was now a whisper in my ear.

"Maybe I can do something to make up for the dreams you gave up for my sake. I've seen and participated in a lot of ugliness, Jaina. You're my refuge from those who would never forgive me, who would never accept this world. But I never, ever want you to inherit my baggage. I will spend every single day of what remains of my life to protect you from my burdens."

"Alex …"

"I just want you to be safe, Jaina. For you to be free. No matter what it takes. If the world can't grant you that, if it tries to punish you for what I've done, that's a world I will never accept."

"So that's what this is all about, huh?" I sighed. "Even after everything that's happened, you're just … worried about me."

"Yes, Jaina. I am worried about you."

I smiled. "Okay then. I accept it."

"Jaina …?"

"I accept your protection, Alex. I'll allow you to take care of me. Do whatever you want to ensure my safety and freedom."

"Just like that?"

"Of course, silly." I giggled and kissed her eagerly. "I love you, remember? Of course, I'll support you in fighting for the things you care about! Even if the thing in question is, well, me."

"Jaina, you truly are amazing!"

Alex eagerly ushered me into the bedroom. She pushed me flat on my back and began undressing me in earnest.

"I'm all yours for the taking. Use me however you like!"

"That was always the plan." I smiled playfully, "But since you're so eager, I'll let you take the lead this time."

Alex responded by sinking her face into my chest, and I started feeling very ticklish from the relentless kisses she was planting all over my body.

"You're a good girl," I whispered as Alex continued to indulge herself. "You're an amazing girl. You're my favorite girl."

She shifted positions, feeling me up from behind. And all the while, I felt so happy that she had embraced her desires, that she was enjoying herself so much.

"And always remember, Alex. You deserve to be happy."

Above All Else

"Alex …" I murmured, as she continued to ravish me.

"I love you. I love you, I love you …" she murmured as she finished undressing me.

I felt overwhelmed, but also curious. What had happened to her? Why was she being so eager, so … desperate to make love to me like this?

I couldn't really get the opportunity to ask though. Alex was being incredibly aggressive, and my body was very tempted to just give in to the desire that was building up within me. And so, give in I did.

"Aaaah! Oooh!" I moaned as I felt the pleasure of our union, even as Alex continued to love me.

All my doubts went away and I was just happy. Happy for the moment, happy she was with me, happy that I felt so, so good.

I could feel the drowsiness kick in as we finished, and my body relaxed.

"Alex ..." I murmured.

"Shh," she said, caressing my hair. "Relax, babe. You're safe. You're okay. Just stay in my arms. Let me protect you."

"Okay, but ..."

She cut me off with a kiss as her body pressed closer to mine.

"Just relax, and smile. Smile for me, Jaina."

"Alex ... you're so beautiful," I said as I smiled. "You're the best thing that's ever happened to me."

"Jaina ..." was she choking back tears? "You're everything to me. Everything. I will protect you. I will make you happy. No matter the cost."

I was fast asleep before I could think about it anymore.

Alex's Story

I finally let my tears flow once I was certain that Jaina was in deep sleep. I couldn't let her worry. I couldn't let her see me so lost, so despondent. Not after everything she'd sacrificed for me.

I would never let my precious Jaina suffer because of my problems.

I heard a knock on the door, and hurriedly put on my nightrobe before opening it.

Gabby was waiting on the other side.

We drove to the meeting point. I was wearing the latest Stellaris-issued battle armor, which was a black tactical jumpsuit, all the better to conceal myself. Gabby would be the one talking to the bastards who dared to threaten Jaina's dream. I would decide whether they walked out of the meeting alive.

Gabby stopped near the water tower. The sniper rifle was strapped to the back holster of my suit. I got out and faced the vantage point I needed to climb to.

"I'll keep them talking. Whether they live or die, is entirely your call, Alex."

"Thank you for this, Gabby."

"Don't mention it. Nobody messes with Stellaris, or its people, on my watch."

She got back in the car and drove on. I began to climb.

At the top of the tower, I looked through the scope of my sniper rifle. Gabby was waiting for our targets, who finally came.

Two people, a man and a woman, got out of a jeep and approached her.

"Derek's not here?" the man, Jason, said.

"I'm afraid he's a little preoccupied at the moment," Gabby said.

I'd already tortured him to death and disposed of the body. He was the one who'd planted the charges on Jaina's orphanage, after all.

What remained to be seen was how complicit his associates were in his scheme.

The woman, Janet, said, "Never mind. We'll get in touch with him later. In any case, you're the backup, aren't you?"

"That I am," Gabby said, playing her part perfectly. "But to be frank, I wasn't comfortable with how far he went. Bombing an orphanage would've buried us. What was he thinking?!"

"Calm down, Gabby," Janet said. "The charges would've been set off when the building was empty. We have no interest in civilian casualties."

"Indeed, our only intent was to send a message to that class traitor. Jaina fought by our side among the Lightwardens, but she's turned her back on everything she stood for! We could never abide by an orphanage running under Stellaris control!"

"So, that was the sole objective?" Gabby said. "To destroy the orphanage because of its Stellaris connections?"

"Yeah," Janet said. "I'm sorry spies like you are always kept in the dark, but we have our reasons. But yes, your concerns are valid and deserve to be addressed. We would never try to kill anyone who isn't Stellaris scum. This whole operation was meant to save the orphans from being corrupted into Stellaris loyalists."

"So that's it? That's why you wanted to bomb the orphanage? To ensure that they couldn't grow up under Stellaris influence?"

"That's right. That's why we ordered Derek to set the charges. We would've made sure to avoid any collateral damage. I hope our position is clear to you now. So, will you help us?"

"Fuck you," I said and shot them both in quick succession.

"Does that answer your question?" Gabby said, gloating at the dead bodies before her. I saw her kneel and rummage through their belongings.

I climbed down the water tower, and soon after saw Gabby pull in.

"Excellent job, Alex. You gave those bastards the death they deserved."

"It was too quick," I muttered. "If I could, I'd …"

"Hey." She rested her hand on my shoulder. "They're not worth it. I've scanned their bodies already, and I know where the resistance group is based in. We can end this, here and now."

"Then let's do it," I said. "Leave no one alive."

"Absolutely." Gabby smiled. "I'll alert the standby team, but you'll have to lead them. Think you're up for it, Chief of Security?"

A bloodthirsty smile crept across my lips. I'd killed a lot of people, mostly with indifference, sometimes with regret.

But this time was different.

"With pleasure."

The bloodbath was over quickly. The resistance bastards didn't stand a chance against the sharp finesse of the Stellaris strike team that vanquished them. Especially since it was a team I'd trained myself.

I may have been more hands-off as of late in order to lighten my workload and spend more time with Jaina, but I never let myself get rusty. I would regularly train myself, and Stellaris security agents to make sure we retained our edge against those who would threaten us. And I had no issues taking up the Chief of Security mantle again, now that Jaina had been threatened.

There is no line I wouldn't cross to protect her. She was the love of my life, and making her smile was what I cared about above all else. If anyone would endeavor to take that smile away from her, I would make them pay.

It had been such a struggle to get Stellaris to fund the orphanage Jaina wanted to run. It had been so hard for me to engineer a balance both Stellaris and her would be satisfied with. But I did it all for her, and nobody who dared to tread on her dreams deserved to live.

After returning home, I immediately undressed myself, hid away the jumpsuit and sniper rifle, and got back into bed with my beloved. I smiled and caressed her body as I lay next to her, watching her sleep. She would wake up happy, refreshed, and eager to tend to the family she'd created. And I'd do whatever I needed to protect her.

I could feel the sunlight nudging me awake the next morning, alongside what felt like kisses down my body.

I woke up to see a smiling Jaina gently kissing me wherever she could.

"Oh." She smiled bashfully as her eyes met mine. "So, you're awake."

"That's right!" I said, and aggressively pulled her in for a nice, big smooch.

"Oh, Alex!" She giggled. "God, I love you so much."

I pulled her close and held her as firmly as I could, caressing her hair.

"I love you too, baby. I'm so, so happy that you're in this world."

"Mmm … maybe I should leave the orphanage to the staff this time and just spend the day with you."

I smiled at her and kissed her deeply in response. "Yeah, let's do that Jaina. The whole day, just the two of us. I'll take care of calling in the staff."

I'd tell them to make sure that all evidence of the attempted bombing was cleared out. Jaina didn't need that weighing down on her.

"Um, Alex …" a look of concern passed over her face. "Are … are you okay?"

"Jaina, I …" I continued to move my hands down her hair. "I am now. I'm more than okay."

What was that I sensed in her eyes? Apprehension? Worry? No, she didn't need to worry about me.

"Alright," she said. "Call the staff in. I'll just freshen up."

"Okay." I kissed her, and she got up and headed for the bathroom.

I grabbed my phone and made a call.

"Hello, Kyle?"

"Yes, Mrs Vander?"

"Has the evidence of the attempted bombing been scrubbed?"

"Yeah. The orphanage will be back to business like nothing ever happened."

"Okay. Resume operations. Jaina needs some time off, so I expect you to manage things in her stead. And Kyle, should any suspicious people poke around the place, detain them immediately. I'll personally interrogate them if I have to."

"Understood. So long, Mrs Vander."

As he hung up, I put away the phone … and saw Jaina staring right at me.

"O … oh …" I froze in place. "J-Jaina … I … I'm …"

She quickly closed the distance between us and kissed me.

"Hey … what are you …"

"I don't care ..." she whispered and kissed me again.

"Jaina?"

"I don't care what you've done." She wrapped her arms around me and pushed me back onto the bed. "You didn't have to hide anything from me. I would've understood, Alex."

"Jaina ... I ..." I choked up, and I could feel the tears starting to flow. "I'm sorry. I'm so sorry ..."

Her smile was so warm. So comforting. It was as though she'd seen right through me, and yet she loved me just as much as she always had.

"It's okay, Alex. It's all going to be okay."

I surrendered to her warmth. Her comforting touch. And I just let myself go. I cried, and cried, not even being able to put into words what I was feeling. And she kept holding me. Kept smiling at me.

"I ... I lied to you ... I broke your trust. I ... I didn't want you to know the things I'd done ... You don't have to forgive me, Jaina."

"But I do forgive you. I'll always forgive you. No matter what."

"D ... do I deserve it ...?"

"Alex …" she smiled as she caressed my cheek. "I've chosen you. I want you to follow your dreams, fulfil your vision, and do what you think is necessary. I want you to be happy."

"E … even if it goes against everything you stand for?"

"I told you, my love." She kissed me. "That doesn't matter anymore. My doubts, my ideals, my convictions … none of them were worth losing you. I know you have your way of doing things, your own way of looking at the world. And I made the choice to live by that because I wanted to be with you. You have nothing to worry about."

"Jaina, I … I keep thinking about everything I've done to you. How I kept pushing on despite your doubts about Stellaris … always doing what I felt like. And I did it again … I never even talked to you about what happened with your orphanage. I just reacted all on my own … keeping you in the dark. I didn't stop. I never stopped. How can I claim to love you when I've only ever done things my way?"

"Because I'm still happy with you, Alex. You're headstrong, you're stubborn, you never back down once you've made up your mind about something. People like you are the ones who'll decide the future of this world, for better or worse. And I've accepted that."

"Jaina ... are you seriously ... all right with this?" I was afraid now. Afraid of how much I'd changed her. My beloved Jaina, the beautiful, idealistic woman that I'd fallen in love with ... just what had I done to her?

"Well, I am conflicted. I've often had to struggle with the conflict between your dreams and what I thought was the right thing to do. Day after day I wondered if it was worth accepting the world people like you were building when I could see so much wrong with it. Even after I revealed my doubts to you, I realized time and again that your and my ideals could never fully align. But despite all that, you know what I wanted more than anything else, Alex?"

"Jaina ..."

"I wanted to be with you! I wanted to make you happy! And if my ideals would get in the way of having a future with you, I'd let them go. And that's why I'll always stand by you, Alex. I want to be the one you can lean on. I want to be the one who loves you, day after day. Because spending my days with you, living by your side ... I'll give up anything to keep doing that!"

"I'm sorry I lied to you." I leaned in and kissed her ferociously. "And I'm sorry for all the pain I've put you through. But I'm so grateful, Jaina. I'm so grateful you chose me. To think … that I could ever matter so much to anyone … oh God!"

I held her as close as I could as I let my emotions overtake me. It was all so overwhelming. The guilt of having lied to her. The regret of not doing enough for her. But more than anything, I felt gratitude for being so important to her. For meaning so much to the woman I loved more than anyone else.

And so, my tears flowed free, and my cries reverberated across the room. Someone who accepted me and treasured me so dearly was someone I never, ever wanted to let go of.

My precious Jaina would never be alone as long as I drew breath.

An Oath to Commemorate

I was still coming to terms with the fact that this was actually happening.

We'd already been together for so many years, but Alex had a better memory than I gave her credit for. And she was clearly more sentimental than she gave herself credit for.

After all this time, she proposed to me. On her knees, with a wedding ring, asking me to marry her.

The only reason I hesitated for a small moment to say yes was because I was so taken aback to be even asked this question.

She looked ecstatic as she slipped the ring on my finger, and hugged me fiercely.

"Thank you, Jaina! Thank you, thank you thank you!"

"Just look at you, Alex. After all this time, you actually want a wedding?"

"I know, I know. I was the one who kept implying we didn't need one. But I … I just want to remind myself how special you are, Jaina. I need to make the effort to acknowledge just how lucky I am to be with you."

"And this was the day you swept me off my feet and declared me your princess all those years ago, isn't it?"

"Yeah …" She chuckled in embarrassment. "So you remember that, huh?"

"You're damn right," I said as I leaned in to kiss her.

I could sense her longing for me by just how aggressively she kept kissing me over and over again. I wasn't complaining though.

"God, I love you. I love you so, so much," she murmured as we kept making out.

"So, Alex," I murmured, "How far have you planned our wedding?"

"I'm not sure. I'll discuss it with my friends at work." Alex said, "But I kinda want to hold the ceremony in the orphanage."

"Huh? In front of all the kids? Why?"

"I mean, since I'm like one of their mothers, alongside you, I just wanted to show them what two people do when they really love each other. Maybe it'll make them feel more like a family, you know?"

"You … you're a good person, you know that?" I smiled as I caressed her hair. "Ever since I spoke about it out loud, you've really pushed me to make my dream of raising all those kids a reality. I'm glad I could make that dream come true, Alex."

"Well, I'm glad you let me in," she said as she kissed me. "When it came to having all these children to raise, I was wondering if you'd want me to influence them, given who I work for, and …"

"Just stop, Alex," I said, firmly. "You deserve to be their mother. You are their mother. They need to learn from you. I don't ever want to hear you beating yourself up about this just because you work for Stellaris."

"But maybe if I hadn't involved myself, then no one would have targeted the orphanage, and … and part of me always thought that you wanted to teach those kids to be free from Stellaris influence. And it's not like I haven't been responsible for orphaning children myself ..."

"I already told you, didn't I? None of it matters to me. You're my lover. My fiancée. There's no way I'd ever start a family without you."

"I know." She nodded. "I'm sorry, Jaina. All this self-pity must be exhausting for you, right?"

"No, dealing with it is just part of my duty, isn't it? My duty as your princess. I know the grave circumstances a knight like you can find yourself in. Everything you've been burdened with ... it must've made you feel so lost. Maybe even alone. That's why you can always come into my arms when you return."

"Yeah, you're my princess. My princess who I'll always protect. Despite everything, I still get to come home to your smile. I want to keep that smile alive, Jaina."

I kissed her. "Knowing that you're with me, that I can love you and treasure you, that's more than enough to make me smile, Alex."

"God, you mean so much to me," Alex said as she hungrily kissed me again. "We'll show our children what love is. We'll help them grow up into wonderful people."

"Yes we will, Alex. We'll raise a wonderful family together. Let's give them a wedding to remember, okay?"

"Yeah, okay."

The One I Uplifted

"Are you truly that surprised to hear this?" Becca said as I stared blankly ahead.

"No," I muttered. "No. As a Vander, I could see the signs, but hearing it spoken plainly … it's still a lot to take in."

To think we had gone this far already. The sheer extent of how much we'd reshaped the very fabric of reality left me speechless.

"It's because of *her*, isn't it? You're still worried about what that self-righteous rebel thinks," Vincent said, his sharp tone catching me off-guard.

"Vincent!" Becca stared at him accusingly.

"No point in beating around the bush. We both know Alex has a … conflict of interest here. You don't think your precious Jaina will take kindly to learning about our grand designs, do you?"

I glared at him, furious. Because I knew he was right. "I know, Vincent. I know she won't like this. No need to rub it in."

"Then tell me, Alex. What are you going to do about it?"

I was already tense enough, but now I could really feel the pressure. I'd already promised Jaina that I'd protect her, even if she rebelled again. And I meant it. No matter what, I wanted to come home to her smile, her warmth, her kisses.

But serving Stellaris had always been my destiny. Ever since I was a child, I knew I had to seize it. To become one of the chosen, to become the brightest star in the Vander lineage.

And I was so close now. So, so close. But if the price I had to pay was truly so steep, then …

"You don't want to choose, do you?" Becca's soft, comforting voice instantly melted away my worries.

"Becca …?"

She closed the distance between us and put her hand on my shoulder.

"You want it all, right Alex? Your destiny, and your love. You don't want to settle for anything less, do you?"

"N-no …" I murmured. "Not if I can help it."

I could feel her arms wrap around me, as she pulled me into an embrace.

"Then get them both, Alex. Take it all."

"Take it all …?"

"Exactly. You're going to take the new world for yourself, and you're going to bring Jaina into it, and she's going to smile and take your hand as you do. You are going to turn her, Alex."

"Would … would that really work?"

"Can you accept any other outcome?"

"No …" I murmured, my resolve hardening. "No, I can't. Jaina will come around. I'll make sure of it. I'm going to love her with all my heart, and she's going to live in our new world! I will have it all!"

"Yes, that's my girl!" Becca yelled. "We're going to have it all! Everything we want! Because that's who we are!"

"HELL YEAH!" I yelled.

Just then, as I looked around, I noticed that Vincent had gone.

"Where's Vincent?" I murmured.

"He doesn't matter. You don't need his approval or his permission. You just need to prove that this world belongs to you, Alex. Are you ready to do that?"

"I am," I said, looking resolutely into Becca's eyes. "One day, both Jaina and I will take our rightful place in this world. I promise you."

"That's just what I wanted to hear," Becca said. Her smile was so warm. So comforting. But also invigorating. Inspiring.

Yes. I could do it. I could do anything.

Jaina and I would rule the world together. I'd make sure of that, no matter how long it took.

And once Jaina finally joined me, I'd tell her everything. I couldn't wait for the day when there were no more secrets, no more conflicts.

The Honeymoon

"Do you, Alex Vander, take Jaina Marshall to be your lawfully wedded wife?"

"I do."

"And do you, Jaina Marshall, take Alex Vander to be your lawfully wedded wife?"

"I do."

"By the power vested in me by the Gods above, I now pronounce you partners in life, be it sickness or health. You may now kiss."

And kiss we did. And the children clapped, overjoyed to see their mothers tie the knot. We'd just shown them the strength of our commitment to each other, and it was now time to live up to the example we were setting.

It gave me a strange feeling. Something warm, and joyous unlike anything I'd truly felt before. It was not a feeling I was ever going to forget.

It was also not lost on me that even though Alex had wanted this wedding be conducted in front of the children just so we could deepen our bond with them, we were also going to take a long sabbatical from running the orphanage because of it. We really wanted that honeymoon with each other, after all.

Alex promised me this around-the-globe trip where it would be just the two of us witnessing the earthly pleasures the Stellaris Coalition had to offer to us. And I gave into my hedonistic impulses and accepted her idea without hesitating.

But while experiencing new places would be a fresh and stimulating experience on its own, what I truly longed for, above all else, was all the alone time I would get with my beloved Alex. I wanted this time with her, to really be with her, understand her, and connect with her. With nothing else getting in the way.

And on the first night of our honeymoon, I would feel the ravenous longing she had for me as she gorged herself on my body, her hunger unmatched even by my lust for her. On many days, I'd pushed back to claim my own desires, my own strength. But this time, I submitted myself to her appetite, knowing that being consumed by her was its own reward.

Awash in the pleasure, I allowed Alex to hold me as tightly as she could, her lips still eagerly peppering my body with kisses. Yes, I truly did feel like a plaything today. A plaything who'd been pushed to her limits.

And when I heard the joyful moans from my beloved, I knew it had all been worth it.

"We're going to be like this day after day, babe. There's nothing else in our way now. You're all mine, and I'm all yours."

"Yeah." I smiled and kissed her fiercely, a feeble attempt to assert my own strength after being so thoroughly dominated. "Thank you … for not being gentle. It was fun."

A playful, but also vicious, chuckle rang out. "Well, glad to hear it, my love. I only hope you can put up a better fight next time."

"Maybe," I said, still awash in the afterglow as I kissed her and savored her. I no longer had any sense of the time passing around me.

There was only her body, and my desire to enjoy it.

Our appetites did eventually subside, as appetites do, but the warmth and joy we felt around each other felt pervasive, as though it was this beautiful aura surrounding us. It felt so … magical, to be so close to someone that you felt like you could reach out and cradle their very heart whenever you wanted to.

"Hey, Jaina … I've been thinking."

"What is it?" I said and kissed her in the very next breath.

"You've told me that if there was a conflict between me and your ideals, you'd choose me. And that felt so comforting to hear, it really did, but … but it made me wonder."

"Wonder what?" I whispered as I buried my face into her chest.

"About all the times I saw people whose ideals conflicted with mine … and how I destroyed them without a second thought."

My playful smile faded away as I decided to adopt my 'caring Jaina' demeanor. It seemed that, once again, Alex wanted to wrestle through some dilemmas of her conscience with me, so I perked up my ears and hardened my gaze to let her know I was paying attention.

"Back when I was coordinating the expansion of Stellaris, we faced resistance from a number of fanatical factions. They'd seized control of their own little corners of the continent and were content to be left alone … until my forces marched in. And you know what I saw, Jaina?"

"What?"

"People hanging from trees. Women who were flayed and had their … uteri gouged out. Public executions that were cheered on. And everyone thought it was normal. I could see happy families just prancing about and treating the ghastliness around them as if it was no big deal. I'd sometimes conduct recon undercover and ask them what they thought of all the dead people around them, and they casually told me that they'd simply faced God's judgment. The women were punished for aborting their pregnancies, and black people, trans people and disabled people were lynched and hanged for daring to defy their place in the so-called divine order. I didn't even want to ask what they'd do to a lesbian like me."

"Oh my God, I'm so sorry …"

"It was so disgusting … so horrific … that when our squads moved in to engage them ... we became rather merciless ourselves. There was … a lot of collateral damage."

"Wait, by collateral damage, do you mean …"

"Y-yes, Jaina … there were so many people who died by my hands … even children! I couldn't restrain myself … not after the evil that I'd witnessed. And when I'd look back at the consequences of what we'd done … I just …"

She tightened her hold on me.

"They remain some of the worst memories I've ever had. I … I actually thought for a while that I couldn't live like a human anymore … that my entire purpose was just to be a weapon for Stellaris to use. The only thing that brought me back from the brink … was you, Jaina."

"Alex …"

"My horror … my hatred turned me into a monster … but at least I'd never been a monster to you. At least I always tried my best to make you … happy."

I could feel the tears touching my skin.

"And you were back at home, ready to welcome me, hold me, love me … and I had to be there for you. I had to protect my humanity … for your sake. That's the only reason I came out of those days with my heart intact."

She pushed my hand deeper into her chest until I could feel her heartbeat.

"So tell me, Jaina. Please tell me I never crossed this kind of line for you. Please tell me that I'm good enough!"

"You … you're not a monster, Alex. I don't think that of you at all. Even after what you've just told me."

"J … Jaina …"

I kissed her, firmly and deeply.

"Maybe if the first time I ever saw you was the day your forces ravaged the Lightwardens, I wouldn't have forgiven you. Maybe I wouldn't have considered you a friend, and I certainly wouldn't have fallen in love with you. But that's not how things turned out, was it? I first saw you as my friend, then my mentor. And finally … the love of my life. And I'm so, so glad that I didn't walk away from you, even when our bond was tested."

I kissed her again.

"I didn't choose you because you were perfect, Alex. I chose you because I know my love will always reach you. You know the one thing I've always noticed every time I've ever been with you?"

"What?"

"You care, Alex! You care about my happiness, about my ideals, about my opinions! You've always wanted to listen, to give me a chance, even if you didn't agree! And more than that, you've loved me over and over again! Do you have any idea how wonderful it feels to know that I matter so much to someone? To know that I can give someone a reason to smile, to hope and to be happy, just by being me? Do you understand what an amazing gift that is?!"

"You are my hope, Jaina. You've been my hope for so long. But did I really treat you with the reverence you deserved? Was I truly grateful enough, for everything that you've done for me?"

"You're holding me right now, Alex. You've made love to me, kissed me, and opened up to me. You don't hesitate to lean on me, and you're more than happy to let me lean on you. All this is more than enough."

"You won't get sick of me?"

"Never."

"Okay. Then I'll hold you, Jaina. I'll hold you as much as I can. Even if you know it, I don't ever want to stop making it clear how precious you are."

"Likewise, Alex. I never want to stop showing how much I love you."

We didn't say another word. We didn't need to. Our bodies handled the rest.

More of You

Jaina. She laughed as she waded into the sea. She looked unbelievably gorgeous in that swimsuit. It made me lust for her more. Made me fantasize about all the kinky getups she could pull off.

Jaina smiled in delight as she sampled the local cuisine. I'd enjoyed such food all my life, but to treat my beloved to such joys gave me a sense of fulfilment I could never have felt had I been on my own.

Jaina was so clingy. And I liked it so much. She never let an opportunity to hold me, kiss me or fondle me slip by. I never even had to tell her how much I longed for her. She would be by my side regardless.

Jaina wanted me to be happy. Every time I smiled I could see the joy on her face. The way she cared about me, the way she adored me … I'd never had anyone feel that way about me before. Others had smiled at me, been polite to me, or even praised me. But her love filled me up in ways no one else could ever come close to. Every time I held her, I felt reluctant to let her go. How could I ever risk losing someone so, so precious to me?

This one honeymoon was not enough. No, even a whole lifetime of my love would not be enough to repay her for how much she'd brightened up my life. But then again, there's no way to repay the sun, the moon or the earth, is there?

Just as the sun always rose to greet a new day, and the moon illuminated our nights, so would Jaina herself paint the canvas of my life with her own colors. And I would treasure them all the same.

"Thank you," I murmured as I savored her body after a full day of playing with her on the beach. After all the light-hearted games we played with each other as the sun shone upon us both, it was time to play the more intimate, sensual game of love during the night.

"Alex …?"

"Thank you, Jaina. Just ... thank you for being a part of my life. Thank you."

My voice, and my body betrayed so many feelings. Love, lust, vulnerability, possessiveness, hunger, neediness. I wouldn't filter myself this time. I'd let it all out. I had faith in my Jaina. I had faith that she could handle it.

"I love you, Alex. So don't stop. Don't hold back. I'm here to feel everything."

Her words only egged me on as I lost myself in my maelstrom of emotions. I continued to explore her body, and she somehow responded in just the right ways to soothe me, to guide me, to help me. And I was happy to be molded by her, taught by her. Loving her was my ultimate redemption, the one reason above all else that allowed me to believe that it was a good thing for me to exist.

Yes, if someone like Jaina could treasure me so much, it must be a good thing that I was born.

And as her affirming whispers were met with the wonderful pleasure from our tryst, I felt so overwhelmingly happy, and grateful. And I held my precious Jaina as close as I could, hoping that my smile could sufficiently convey just how beautiful and amazing she was.

"Alex." She caressed my face. "Remember this moment. Remember how much I love you. Hold on to it, okay?"

"I will. I'll burn into the very depths of my memory, Jaina."

She leaned in and kissed me. "I promise that I'll love you over and over again during our honeymoon. I want your memories with me to become your lucky charm, Alex. I want them to be the spark that pushes you past whatever darkness you may face in the future, no matter how deep it is."

She kissed me again. "I can't promise to be with you every hour of every day, but I want you to carry a part of me with you no matter what. So I'm engraving my talisman for you right now. And from now until the end of this month, I'll continue to keep engraving more and more of them. I will show just how much you deserve to be loved."

"Oh, Jaina ... my precious Jaina ..." I tightened my hold on her. "I want to say you've done enough, but I'm feeling selfish. I ... I think I really could use those talismans of yours. I just hope that you have enough of my love burned into your mind too."

"I do, Alex," she chuckled. "Don't underestimate how much you've already done for me. How much you're still doing for me. Falling in love with you is the best thing that's ever happened to me. I don't even want to think about how my life would've been without you."

"I'm the best thing that ever happened to you? Really?"

"Really!" Jaina said, without a moment of hesitation. "I love you, Alex! I love you so, so, so, so much!"

We eagerly kissed and squeezed each other, as we continued to murmur about how much we loved one another over and over and over and over ... until my consciousness gave way to sleep.

Honey

I stood by the doorway, watching as Alex continued to work out. It was quite a sight to behold, watching her so absorbed and focused that she could not, and did not notice anything else. That's why I could safely admire her without breaking her concentration or embarrassing her.

And she looked so, so gorgeous. Her tank top and sweatpants clung to her figure and accentuated it in all the right ways. Her slender, toned body moved with such elegance and finesse as she did her crunches, pull-ups and push-ups. I was getting such an eyeful of her while she was none the wiser to my voyeurism.

Part of me wanted to jump on her right away and ravish her, while another part of me wanted to just walk away and rub one out, but I knew the patient choice would have the best payoff. I'd watch her, admire her, and eventually she'd stop to take a break or to rest. And that would be my time to strike.

And as I predicted, eventually she slowed down, grabbed a towel and began wiping off her sweat. And that's when she noticed me.

"Jaina? Sorry, I didn't see you there. Did you need something?"

The second she dropped the towel, I whispered,

"You."

And immediately went on the attack.

"Mmph!" Her muffled voice cried out in shock as I grabbed hold of her and forcefully kissed her.

"Wait, Jaina! Now, seriously?"

"Hell, yeah!" I said and leaned in to kiss her again.

"Wait," she murmured after the kiss. "You've been watching me, haven't you? You were standing here the entire time."

And then, her lips curled into a vicious smile.

"Did you like what you saw?"

It was my turn to be caught off-guard as she suddenly lifted me into a bridal carry, practically ran over to our adjoining bedroom, tossed me onto the bed and pounced right on top of me.

"Crap." I giggled. "So much for the element of surprise."

"Indeed," she said and roughly grabbed hold of me as her lips began to kiss down my neck.

"Mmm ... looks like your training regimen's really paying off."

"I'm still a little strung out from all the exercise. This isn't even me at my full strength."

"I know," I said naughtily, and immediately pushed against her until I was the one on top.

"I want to devour you, Alex. I'll be the one who finishes your workout session."

"Then you'd better put in some work yourself. Because I'm not going down without a fight!"

And so, we wrestled and tumbled all over the bed together, each of us trying to sate our hunger and establish our dominance. Alex was stronger than me by several orders of magnitude, but

I was no slouch myself. And I'd hoped that by catching her at her most vulnerable, I could finally dominate her, finally ravish her completely on my terms.

Sadly, that was not to be. In the end, Alex won out, though she was openly panting by the end of it.

"God, you … you put up a good show, Jaina."

"And I'm still no match for you," I said, with a defeated chuckle.

She responded by forcefully kissing me.

"Does that matter? This was my favorite part of the workout, by far!"

I blinked, momentarily taken aback by the compliment.

"Wait, really?"

"Hell, yeah!" She kissed me fiercely. "My regimen's become so monotonous, you know? I feel like I have to dissociate a little every time just to get through it. But you … you enjoyed watching me. You liked it. And that's the best motivation I could ask for!"

She began undressing me and feeling up my body.

"If I knew you were waiting to play with me after I finished working out, I'd have enjoyed it so much more!"

She sank her face into my chest, as her hands and lips savored my breasts.

"But Alex ..." I murmured, "If I watch you every time you work-out, won't that become monotonous too?"

"Oh ..." she paused, "Oh yeah, you're right. But it's not monotonous today, is it?" she said, kissing down my body.

"So surprise me, Jaina. Show up when I least expect it and go on the attack! This moment ... it's like lightning in a bottle! I love you so much!"

I could feel the excitement building up as Alex continued to diligently pleasure me, but I didn't want to come. Not until I'd felt her up and taken her clothes off too.

And it was as if she read my mind, as she stopped just as I was on the verge of climaxing and slid back up until her face was level with mine again.

"Your turn," she whispered, and I eagerly began to indulge myself.

My beloved wife. My beloved protector.

Her body was so luscious, and her heart had such warmth.

And she was all mine to cherish!

It was so enduringly wonderful, to love and to be loved.

Alive

"I love it," I whispered as I stood, overlooking the vista, with Alex by my side.

She hugged me from behind and pulled me close to her.

"Yeah, we really went out of our way to nurture this island. When my team took out the warring factions that had ravaged it, I wanted to give this place a clean slate, you know. Restore the beauty that had been lost. I'd been keeping tabs on the operation, and I wanted to surprise you."

She kissed my neck. "I'm glad you love it, Jaina. That makes me really, really happy."

I could sense her underlying motivation for doing this, and it truly warmed my heart. But

I wanted to show her how I felt. I had to show her. I had to remind her.

And so I turned around and kissed her slowly. "You did a good thing, Alex. Stellaris did a good thing."

"A … a good thing, huh?" I could hear her voice choking up.

I kissed her again. "You're a good person, Alex. You have such a beautiful heart. This place … it shows that. I think its beauty reflects your beauty."

I could hear her sighing in relief, as though a weight had been lifted off her shoulders.

"A good person. Yeah, maybe I am. Maybe it'll all work out."

"We're here, and we're happy, aren't we? I know that you're doing your best, Alex. There's nothing more admirable than that."

"So, you're happy? You're happy to live in this world I tried to create?"

"I am," I said. I didn't qualify my statements with my countless reservations or disagreements with Stellaris. We'd had that conversation so many times already.

What I wanted her to understand, was that even in spite of all that, I loved this world, and I knew she loved it too. And that, in and of itself, was enough.

"I'm glad you're still concerned about me, about everything I've said," I murmured. "I'm glad you're still trying to improve things. But I don't ever want you to feel like you fell short of my standards, Alex. I'll always, always cherish you, no matter what."

She kissed me hungrily as her hands fondled me.

"I'm … I'm happy to hear that, Jaina. It's funny, you know. All my life I'd been so confident, so headstrong and determined. But the closer I've gotten to you, the more I started doubting myself. Wondering how I'd hurt you, disappointed you. Wondering if I was truly worthy of you. I just… want to keep doing right by you, Jaina. It's like a never-ending compulsion, no matter how many times you tell me that I've done enough."

"Why don't you just enjoy yourself?" I said, caressing her cheek. "Just hold me, kiss me, and make love to me as much as you want. Treasure me and pamper me, as you always have. Don't you enjoy showing me your love?"

"I do. God, I enjoy it so much!"

"Then let's keep doing it. Let's keep expressing our feelings for each other. Let's keep building our universe, Alex."

I kissed her, slowly, once more.

"Maybe you just need to channel your feelings a little differently. Instead of constantly trying to prove your worth, just keep loving me. Use me to satisfy your appetite, Alex. I'm right here."

"Yeah. You're right, Jaina. I'll try. I'll try to just … be in love with you, above all else. Let's take this somewhere cozier, shall we?"

"Yeah, let's."

And so we retreated to our cabin, and let loose our overflowing love for each other. Yes, this wonderful cycle was enough for me. For us to affirm each other, love each other, rest with each other, and do it all over again.

The very fact that Alex was alive, and with me, was enough to give purpose and meaning to my life. I could spend my entire lifetime caring for her and learning about her, and there would never be a finish line. There would never come a day when she stopped being the vibrant, complex, beautiful, and *alive* woman she was.

That was the best thing about falling in love. The fact that you had another life to share your days with. To care for. To be cared for by. And life was always full of discoveries, new depths, and new puzzles. You just had to know where to look.

And as I climaxed in joy, and heard the pleasurable moans of Alex, I held on to her and felt her chest rise and fall with each breath, her heartbeat at regular intervals, the warmth only the skin of a living human being could have. And I feasted on her body, this living, evolving shell that housed my beloved's soul.

My love would be nourished and sustained by nothing other than the very fact that Alex was a living, breathing person. And her worth to me was infinite.

"Live," I whispered to her. "Live, Alex. That's all I want from you."

"Alright," she said, as we kissed each other, our bodies completely intertwined. "Then you do the same, okay? Live as much as you can."

Our murmurs gave way to us simply enjoying each other. Simply … being.

Determination

Alex was smiling lazily as I continued to kiss her.

"It was worth it, you know. It was all worth it. I'm so glad we did this honeymoon."

"Yeah," I whispered as I continued savoring her body.

Her hands were wrapped around my body. She was holding me close, and firm. I knew that she'd never let go of me anytime soon. And I was glad.

I slowly, gently unbuttoned her blouse and began kissing down her exposed chest. She'd been surprisingly passive this time, letting me take the lead. But the strength of her grip was how I knew that she was still as powerful as ever.

"Thank you, Jaina. I managed to clear up all these cobwebs in my mind that I didn't even know were there. All because you were here for me."

"I know. You've opened up a lot to me. I'm glad I was a good listener."

Her hands suddenly moved to my cheeks, as she held my face firmly and gazed into my eyes.

"This world is mine to rule. I'm going to make sure it's worthy of you. I'll leverage everything Stellaris has in order to keep you happy, and safe."

"Alex ..." I paused. This sudden show of determination had caught me off-guard.

"Don't worry, Jaina. I'm not going anywhere. I don't need to. Everything I need to do, I can do by your side. But my purpose is so clear now, you know? As clear as it was when I first joined Stellaris. I will make sure this world belongs to you, no matter what."

"What ... what do you mean by that?"

"It means I'll grant your every wish. Your every desire. And I don't care who gets in the way of that. Just tell me about the world you want to live in, and I swear I'll make it a reality! I can do it, Jaina. I know I can."

"Alex, please … the world I want is right here. You're right here. You've already done it. You've already created a world for me. For us."

"I … I know," Alex said, seemingly calming down. "I'm sorry, Jaina. I just got a little carried away. I didn't mean to put so much pressure on you."

Before I could respond, she leaned in and kissed me. Slowly. Deeply.

"I really should do better at living in the moment," she said with a sheepish smile as she pulled back. "I just can't help myself from overthinking, can I?"

"Alex …"

I didn't doubt her words. I didn't doubt she was telling me the truth.

But it wasn't the whole truth. I could feel the steely determination from her still. I knew that something had awakened within her. She hadn't forgotten her plans. She was just changing them, adapting them.

And that scared me. That had always scared me. The things Alex had done when driven by her determination had left me conflicted, worried, even despondent. The way she relentlessly tried to reshape the fabric of the world to fit her desires, no matter the consequences. The way she was always reaching out into the unknown, the uncertain.

I had sometimes wondered if she was even doing the right thing. But now my worries were different. All I cared about was protecting her, staying by her side. But if her mission consumed her, would I truly lose her for good? Would she finally cross a line she couldn't come back from? And what would that do to her?

"Hey, Jaina ..." I heard her whisper, as she suddenly kissed me.

"Please don't worry, Jaina," she whispered, as she kissed me again. It was as if she was trying to hypnotize me.

"I love you. I will always love you. I will never, ever leave you alone. I will always be with you." Another kiss. I couldn't keep my thoughts straight anymore. She knew, didn't she? She'd seen right through me.

"I will stay with you as long as you want me to. You can have me whenever and wherever you want. That will never change."

"I ... I know, Alex. But still ..."

Another kiss.

"You don't have to be afraid, Jaina. I'll face the unknown for you. I'll brave the hardships for you. I'll never let anyone hurt you. And I'll never let anyone take you away from me."

"R-really? I'm … not going to lose you?"

"No."

She was undressing me now, her firm hands quickly pushing me to the bottom of the bed.

"How can I hope to create a world for you if I'm not with you? How can I hope to keep you happy if I lose you? And how could I ever disregard the pleas and wishes that you have made?"

"Alex … nothing lasts forever … not even us …"

"Do you want it to?"

I looked at her piercing gaze. Her hardened expression. She was deadly serious. Whatever I wanted, she would make it her life's mission to grant it to me.

"I … I don't care. I really … really don't," I murmured. "All I want, is to love you in the moment. But thinking about the future … it scares me."

"I already told you. I'll face the unknown for you, my love."

"But it's not that simple!" I yelled. "I won't stop worrying just because you protect me from everything! Even if you say that you'll be okay … that you'll never leave me … I can't be sure of that! I can't be sure of what happens if you fail, or if something outside of our control happens, and …"

"Jaina …"

"I … I'm worried about you too, Alex! I want to protect you! You've always put yourself in danger, always run forward and tried to change the world, and all I can think about is how things won't be the same anymore, and that maybe one day, you won't be around to love me, and ... and …"

I burst out sobbing.

"And there's nothing I can do to keep you safe! Because you're always taking the lead! Always charging ahead! I just have to rely on your word. Your word that you won't go anywhere. Your word that you'll always stay with me. And that's all I can do, isn't it? Just put my faith in you that everything will be alright! Nothing more!"

She'd already taken me into her arms, as I was crying into her chest. She didn't say a word. She just gently caressed me. Patted me. Kept me warm.

It took some time before I could stop feeling overwhelmed. Where had that outburst even come from? Just what had gotten over me?

"Jaina, you've saved me so many times over. You really have. I owe so much to you."

"Alex … I … I'm sorry …"

"No, don't apologize. You have every right to feel the way you do."

"I … I must have really left you confused, huh?"

"It doesn't matter. I'm here to listen to you. To understand you."

She gently pulled back, caressed my cheek, and kissed me.

"Relationships go both ways, and I think I got a little too caught up in myself this time. I was so assured of my feelings, of my mission, that I couldn't empathize with you properly. I'm sorry about that."

"No, don't say sorry Alex, it's not your fault!"

"Okay. I won't blame myself. But I want you to understand something. I need you. I need you a lot. I wouldn't be the woman I am today if I didn't have you to lean on. To protect me."

"I … protected you?"

"Yes! You've protected me from my inner demons, from naysayers. Even physical danger. There were so many times when just thinking about you tempered my recklessness. Every time I was in a dangerous situation, I made it a point to protect myself, so that I could come home to you."

"I … I get it. I just … I just wish I could protect you from being in danger in the first place. You try to take on so much, and I wish I could take some of that burden off you."

"Jaina …"

We kissed again.

"You're so good at talking to me, you know? You're very honest about your doubts, your fears, and your hopes. And you're so attentive in listening to mine. I feel safer around you than I do with anyone else. Even myself, in fact."

"Alex …"

"It's so comforting, knowing that I don't have to be alone with my thoughts. That I can come to you any time and you'll always listen. You have never, ever let me down when I needed you, Jaina."

I pulled her closer, sinking my face deeper into her chest.

"And I can be so free around you, you know? I can talk about my fantasies of princesses, knights, magic, and the universe we're building! It's easier for me to be a child around you than it was when I was a child in my own family! I had no idea what I was missing out on! What I was burying deep inside me, both good and bad! But you set me free!"

I didn't know what to say. I just felt so happy. How easy it was for me to forget just how much I'd helped her.

"And that's why I feel so determined! So strong! Because I've had you nurturing me all these months, with no interferences! There is nothing more wonderful to me than your love, Jaina, and you've loved me relentlessly day after day! It's only because of you that I feel so amazing! My strength, my power is only there because you nurtured it. You're already my armor."

"Alex … I love you so much …"

"Jaina …" We kissed. "Can you keep protecting me?"

"Yeah." I smiled. "I'll protect you with everything I have!"

"Good." She began kissing my body, as my desire for her returned in earnest. "Because I can't do this without you."

"Yeah." I smiled as I ravished her once more. "We'll rule this world together, Alex. As equals."

"Yeah. Equals," she murmured. God, she was so amazing. So wonderful. She was everything I wanted, and I was everything she wanted.

We could do it. I knew that now. We could create a world just for us, where all our dreams would come true no matter who got in our way.

And it was going to be so beautiful.

Interview

I sat across from Becca as she sized me up. Alex had put in a good word for me, and now it was time to cross the Rubicon.

I was going to join Stellaris. I was going to embrace Alex's world, as an equal.

This was where I let go of my old self forever.

"So, Jaina Marshall, you've finally decided to come around. Finally decided to follow our mission."

"Yes, ma'am." I nodded stiffly.

"No need to be so formal, Jaina. You don't have to stand on ceremony after how frank you've been with me. That's not why I'm interviewing you."

"Then what is it you want to know?"

"I wanted to confirm one thing, and I wanted to hear it straight from you. You're doing this for Alex, aren't you?"

I hesitated for a bit, my instinctive need to keep up appearances stopping me from confirming the truth right away. But I knew this conversation would go nowhere if I didn't give an honest answer.

"Yes," I sighed. "I'm doing this for Alex. I'm doing this so that we can create a new world, just for the two of us."

Becca's smile widened, the warmth in her eyes making me drop my guard.

"That's all I wanted to hear. You want to know what the true purpose of Stellaris is, Jaina?"

"Stellaris is a megacorporation, isn't it? You want to dominate the marketplace, make sure your position is assured."

"Yes, but market dominance, profit maximization, keeping shareholders happy, these are all just means to an end, you know. Stellaris will ensure its economic and political supremacy at all costs, but we're doing it in service of one clear goal."

"One goal? What is this goal?"

Becca smiled knowingly, "To make the dreams of the worthy come true."

"The ... worthy?"

"Yes," Becca said. "The people who have inherited or earned Stellaris's favor. That includes the top management, such as the Board of Directors, and the Executive Leadership, which I'm a part of, and which Alex was a part of. And lastly, there's the Advisory Board, which looks toward the horizon, planning out our long-term prospects. All of us are the chosen ones, the stewards of the current world order. And it's a world order that exists only to fulfil our wishes."

"Your wishes?"

"Indeed. We will make the world cater to our desires. The rest of humanity will be the tools we use to satisfy our cravings. Everyone beneath us exists only to serve our whims. Everywhere we go, the world transforms to accommodate our wants and needs. That is the true power of Stellaris's chosen ones!"

"And Alex was a chosen one? Was she ... one of you the entire time?"

"Of course!" Becca laughed. "As a scion of the Vanders, she had a path cleared to the upper echelons from the very beginning! All she had to do was prove her competence and her loyalty, and eventually, she'd have the power to create her own world! And we thought we had a pretty good idea of what that world would be. That is, until she met you."

"Me?"

"Yes, you. The rebel who clung to the old-fashioned ideas of justice. The rebel who kept worrying about the needs of the many, and desiring justice for all. The fact that Alex fell in love with you was somewhat ... disruptive."

"Disruptive?"

"Yes. In all honesty, she was relatively soft-hearted from the start, far more in tune with the commoners than she really needed to be. And thanks to you, she really began to question some of our methods and practices. It was a bit of a challenge to properly initiate her, until we realized how you were a blessing in disguise."

"I ... I was a blessing?"

"Indeed. The answer was so simple when we pieced together the common thread. The one commonality that ran through all of Alex's doubts, reservations and concerns. That commonality was your happiness. And if all we had to do was make you happy, that was hardly an issue!"

"You … you made me happy?"

"Not quite," Becca said. "We can't manipulate emotions on a consistent basis, and we can't really target individual people. The results are far too unpredictable. What we can do, however, is shape your environment. And so we created a world that you'd want to live in, a world where you could lose yourself in Alex's love and live a happy carefree life! Alex loved you so much, understood you so well, that it was a cakewalk to create that paradise for you!"

"You … you created my world? All of you've … been manipulating me this entire time? Even Alex?!"

"Jaina, relax." Becca softened her tone. "We never lied to you. We're not in the business of selling fanciful illusions. The paradise, the gift Alex gave you, is very real."

"How can that be? How can you just … create a paradise like that?"

"Because our technology and our products allow us to manifest the will of our chosen ones, Jaina. Everywhere that people use our services, they're conditioned to serve the will of whichever chosen one claims that world. Everywhere Alex has gone, the people have served her and obeyed her because that's how they were programmed. And because you're the love of her life, they've served you too."

"Served me? What are you talking about? I never had anyone at my beck and call. I wasn't using anybody!"

"Oh, Jaina," Becca sighed. "That's your problem. Your outdated way of thinking. Sure, back when Stellaris was struggling for dominance we'd need to subjugate the people from time to time, but that's no longer necessary. You think people serve your will simply by doing as you say? We all know it's not that simple!"

"Then what is it? How did the people serve me?"

"It's simple. They created the kind of world that you wanted to live in, Jaina. They were peaceful. They were polite. They acted as equals. And every time you stood up for them, they were grateful to you, because you were important to them."

"And they've all … been conditioned to be this way? All this time?"

"Well, it's been a process," Becca said. "Like, around the time Alex first met you, we still hadn't finalized the system even in the American Federation. Things were quite unpredictable for some time, no thanks to the Lightwardens." She gave a cheeky smile. "After we successfully dissolved them, however, things went a lot smoother. I think by the time Alex retired as Chief of Security, we'd successfully conditioned the vast majority of the American population."

"So, as Stellaris became more dominant, everyone else was just being controlled? None of them had free will?"

"Not absolute free will, no. Of course, we'd never override anyone's will entirely, that's hugely impractical. But we do condition them so that their thought processes and motivations fall within acceptable parameters. And it's these parameters that are adjusted based on which of our chosen is being served."

"And Alex knew all this time? She was involved in all of this?"

"She was involved, for a long time," Becca said. "Alex loves you so much, Jaina. Of course she'd want to create a world that was perfect for you! You know, she hated fighting in our wars for global expansion, she hated having to gun down the terrorists who refused to accept our new world order. But she persisted because she knew what awaited her at the end. A world where she'd finally be with you, with nothing else in the way."

"But why didn't she tell me? Why did she keep me in the dark?!"

"Because you weren't ready, Jaina," Becca said. "As long as you continued to resist us, we couldn't trust you with our true purpose. Believe me, Alex wanted to tell you so badly, but she understood that the greater needs of Stellaris needed to be considered. She didn't want to risk everything she'd built for you to fall apart, so she waited. Waited for you to come around and fully embrace us. And now that that day has arrived, we have no reason to keep anything from you. You're one of us now, Jaina. You're one of the chosen!"

I remember what I'd said to Alex that day.

"We'll rule this world together, Alex. As equals."

So this was what my words truly signified. This was what it meant to be Alex's equal.

"Becca. If there are so many chosen among us, how do you ensure our wishes don't clash?"

"That's another marvel of Stellaris technology. We've mastered the art of dimensional layering to create our adjacent universes. Once you've been initiated, you'll have the power to secure your own world. Think of it as a node in our multiverse catered entirely to your needs. Of course, ever since Alex was promoted to Chief of Security, you've been living in her world, but once you're initiated, you'll have a say in creating that world. You'll truly be an equal to her."

"So, I can both synergize with Alex's world or create a world of my own?"

"Absolutely! The choice is yours. But remember, we're all part of one united family. We can visit each other's worlds but attempting to seize ownership of another's world is strictly forbidden, and punishable by death. We need to watch out for each other, at all costs, to preserve the system we've built. I hope you don't forget that."

My beloved Alex. My precious Alex. She'd been building this entire world for us, to make us happy. That's why she was so devoted to Stellaris. That's why she staunchly believed in their mission.

"That means you'll have to play your role in defending our system when the time comes. The threat of terrorists and freethinkers including your former associates, still looms large. You were a former Lightwarden, so I know you have it in you to fight. The question is, will you?"

Alex had meant it all so literally. When she said we'd create our own world, our own future. She'd always wanted to own the world itself. To shape it according to her wishes. And once you stepped out of your fairy-tale fantasies, this is what creating your own world looked like. Conditioning the will of the people, so that they subjugated themselves to your own designs.

And that was the destiny I was now on the cusp of accepting.

I looked up and stared Becca straight in the eye.

"Yes. I'll do anything to protect the world Alex and I have created."

"Excellent. Come with me. It's about time we processed you."

Destiny

I looked over the dimensional interface. I could see all the worlds that had been created by Stellaris's chosen. The number of empty slots was noticeably limited. As I suspected, that's why Stellaris had such a tightly curated network of elites. The luxury of creating your own world could only be afforded to a few.

I could visit, but not have admin access to any of the occupied dimensions, except for Alex's. My choices now were to either synergize with Alex's world or to create a new world of my own.

I chuckled, the realization that I could never have been truly free of Alex until this point dawning on me.

Not that I had any desire to leave her.

I immediately chose to synergize with Alex's world, locking me into her dimension. The only way for me to separate from her now would be to petition Stellaris's Board of Directors for a divorce.

I couldn't wait to run back into her arms, but I still had a few things to take care of.

I undressed and put on the black tactical jumpsuit, activating the vacuum seal. The suit closed all around me until it was skintight. This new Stellaris battle uniform design was so sleek. God, I'd love to see Alex wearing this.

I tried out the numerous weapons in the firing range until I was confident in my ability to fire them. I'd lived so much of my life under Alex's protection, but I couldn't let myself get rusty anymore. No, from here on out, I was going to fight by her side as an equal, no matter what it took.

Once I was satisfied, I changed back to my regular clothes and reported back to Becca. A short while later, I took away my Stellaris-issued jumpsuit and weapon pack and headed toward the exit.

Alex was down in the reception area, waiting for me.

"Jaina." She stood up, "I got the notification. You synergized with my dimension. Does that mean Becca told you everything?"

"Yeah. Yeah, she did."

Alex quickly wrapped her arms around me and held me close. "I'm so sorry, Jaina. I've been wanting to tell you everything for so long. Honestly, when you said you were finally going to join Stellaris, I was afraid. I was afraid of how you might take the truth."

She caressed my hair, the relief in her voice palpable.

"I'm so glad you accepted everything. I'm so glad you accepted me."

"I know, Alex." I smiled. "And I know that even if I'd never joined Stellaris, even if I'd left you before all this, you'd have still treated me like an equal. You'd have kept me free, even if this was your world."

"Of course, baby. Of course. No matter what choice you made, I'd have supported you. You're the most important person in the world to me. This universe always belonged to you as well. Today we just made it official."

"Yeah. We did." I said, as I pulled back and kissed her. "I love you, babe. I love you so much. And I'm so happy to be your equal now!"

"Jaina ..."

"And one more thing. On the last day of our honeymoon, you asked me if I wanted our love to last forever. I didn't know what was truly possible back then, but now that I do, my answer is yes, Alex."

"Jaina ..." She smiled and kissed me eagerly. Deeply. "I understand. I'll ... no ... we'll keep our world alive for as long as it takes! This universe will be an eternal bastion of our love!"

"Yes! Our world! Our dream! And I can craft it, and protect it, together with you!"

"Yeah, you can."

The euphoria I felt as we made love that night was unparalleled. Because I finally understood everything. The truth about Alex, about myself, about our destiny. And she understood too.

That this world existed for our love and our happiness alone. And nothing would ever change that.

The sheer joy of drowning in her love. The overwhelming comfort of knowing these days would never end. The catharsis of knowing that I cherished her, I understood her, and I accepted her. The resolve of knowing that I'd always protect her.

And the gratitude of savoring her wonderful body, right here and now.

This was what it meant to have an eternal paradise all to ourselves.

The Orientation

Alex and I were wearing our tactical jumpsuits. We each had a sidearm holstered, but we weren't really on guard. In fact, we had our arms around each other, as Alex excitedly explained Stellaris's conditioning technology to me.

"These look like cell towers, but their true purpose is mood modulation," she said. "Each of them has a range of 20 miles, so it doesn't take that many to bring an entire city under control. Their conditioning capabilities are rather coarse but incredibly effective."

"Yeah, I imagine no population under their influence would ever be able to mount any sort of protest."

"Indeed." Alex smiled and we kissed. "And we already walked past the food processing plants on our way here. Our additives are what truly allow us to fine-tune the conditioning. That's what's turned our city from merely docile, to serene and peaceful."

"Just the kind of place I'd love to live in. And to think you've been managing this all this time, for me."

We kissed again.

"Well, I didn't do much heavy lifting beyond securing Stellaris dominance here. Once I worked with the Board to set up the conditioning infrastructure, everything kind of sorted itself out."

"I see. So about these terrorists and freethinkers ... how are they able to escape the conditioning?"

"Well, some of them are remnants of prior rebel efforts we couldn't fully squash, like the Lightwardens, and might have learned to counteract our conditioning mechanisms. Others might simply be innately resistant to conditioning and have refused mandatory medical therapy to correct that. While you were able to adapt and assimilate into Stellaris's world quite smoothly, these terrorists have simply refused to accept a peaceful path forward. They're an incredibly stubborn bunch. So desperate to retain their free will that they'll destroy everything we've built for it."

She leaned in and kissed me, and the way she tightly held me close showed me just how protective she still was.

"They've orchestrated bombing campaigns on Stellaris property and targeted the lives of Stellaris executives like Becca. You understand why I've shown them no mercy, don't you?"

"Yeah." I caressed her cheek. "And I won't show mercy either. I'll do whatever I have to."

"Jaina ..." she smiled warmly. "I've tried so hard to protect you from this aspect of my life, but to see you so determined to protect this world ... it makes me really, really happy. Thank you for accepting all this."

I kissed her. Slowly. Deeply.

"I love you, Alex. I want to rule this world with you. I'm your equal now, so you can lean on me for anything, got it?"

"Yeah." Her voice choked up. "Yeah, I understand. God, I love you so much!"

Our passion took over as we continued to kiss each other, over and over again. Even after all the time we'd spent together, this felt like a new beginning for both of us. A new journey that I was so overjoyed to take with her.

"Usually, the Coalition's private military police can take care of any threats to the peace, and if they capture freethinkers, they're quickly subjected to enhanced conditioning," Alex said as we were driven back to our home.

"But when it comes to the truly crafty ones, the kind that can evade attention and strike at critical points in our infrastructure, that's where we come in, Jaina. After all, we do have a responsibility to handle some of our world's defenses directly."

"Well, things sure were relaxed today," I said. "I imagine the terroristic threat isn't all that severe?"

Alex smiled. "No, it isn't. We haven't had a single major incident since the plot to bomb our orphanage. It's been quite peaceful for a long time. Still, I have been discussing matters with Becca. I think it might be useful for some of us chosen ones to band together, you know. Form a team. I know that several of my former colleagues have earned worlds of their own. We could form a new Black Ops squad, answerable directly to the top brass. What do you think about that, Jaina?"

I leaned in and kissed her.

"I think it's a great idea, Alex. I'd love it if you could work with your friends again! And maybe I'll join you too. After all, when else will I see you in that skintight jumpsuit?"

I smiled hungrily, not bothering to hide my arousal.

"Well, you do have a point," Alex said with a knowing smile.

Her hands suggestively traced the contours of my body.

"Shouldn't be long until we reach home."

And indeed, once we reached home, we did not hold back.

Alex eagerly pinned me down and fondled me through my jumpsuit. I in turn eagerly felt her up and peppered her with kisses.

Just making love to her like this, with her passion, her intensity and her strength made me realize a wonderful truth.

"I'm married to a BADASS!"

I hungrily pushed her back, eager to establish my own strength. Alex did not let up, and we eagerly undressed each other and explored each other's bodies.

Our passions and lust drove our movements until a sweet euphoria overcame me, just as I heard Alex moaning from her own climax.

"I love you! I love you I love you I love you!" I muttered as I continued to feverishly kiss her and fondle her, the pleasure giving way to comfort, the comfort giving way to drowsiness.

The drowsiness giving way to a peaceful slumber in the arms of my beloved.

Thank You

I ran my hand down Alex's body, making sure to get a good feel of her breasts, and began kissing down her neck.

"Jaina ..." she murmured with a content smile.

"I love you," I whispered. "I love you so, so much."

She faced me and kissed me on the lips. We took our time savoring the moment.

"So tell me," Alex said. "Was I a good knight? Are you happy with your kingdom, my princess?"

I smiled eagerly and wrapped my arms around her. I wanted to hold her as tightly as humanly possible.

"Beyond my wildest dreams! You've given me everything I could've ever wanted! I want these days to last forever, Alex!"

"They will, my love. I'm going to love you over and over and over again. Your body ... your heart ..."

I could feel her lips tickling me all over as she feverishly kissed me.

"I want to ravish you every single day. Making love to you, just talking to you like this ... I just can't get enough of it."

"There doesn't need to be enough. I will grant you whatever wish, whatever fantasy you have, Alex."

"Then tell me I'm your savior. Tell me I'm your hero, your champion."

"You're my savior. You're my hero. You're my champion."

I could feel the arousal building up within, as Alex began to masterfully pleasure me.

"Tell me you love me. Tell me you want me."

"I love you, Alex. And I want you. I want you so badly."

"Can you thank me, Jaina? Are you ... are you grateful for having me in your life?"

This time her tone was a lot more uncertain. A lot more vulnerable. This wasn't a demand. This was a sincere question. A question that belied just the tiniest seed of doubt.

I guess that was my cue to take the lead.

I immediately tightened my grip on Alex and kissed her hungrily.

"Thank you, Alex."

I then began to eagerly kiss all over her body, and aggressively pressured her, letting my passion run loose.

"Thank you for everything! For coming into my life, making my days so special, loving me all these years, creating this whole new world for me! Thank you thank you thank you thank you!"

"Jaina ..." She was feeling overwhelmed now, but I was not about to let up.

"Thank you for being the best thing to ever happen to me! Thank you for showing me how special I am! Thank you for giving meaning to my life! Thank you for your amazing body! For the wonderful pleasure I feel whenever I make love to you! For your luscious lips, your priceless smile, your joy, your conviction, your everything! Thank you thank you thank-AAAAAAH!"

I climaxed in glee as I felt the euphoria envelop my body, and override my senses. Within seconds, I could feel Alex's grip tighten on me as she moaned in pleasure herself.

"Oh! Oh! Oh! Ooooh …"

My passion gave way to a pervasive pleasure that warmed my body, as I held on tightly to my beloved Alex.

She leaned in to kiss me on the lips.

"I suppose you can't have faith without doubt," she muttered. "Thank you for indulging me, Jaina. What you just did … it meant a lot."

"If you ever need me to indulge you again, all you have to do is ask, my love. I want to serve you. I want to help you."

"Yeah, I know," Alex said, burying her face into my chest. "Whenever I need you, I'll do my best to let you know."

I smiled and caressed her hair. Yes, this is what heaven must be like. A collection of beautiful, intimate moments I could simply lose myself in.

As long as we were here to love each other, we wanted nothing else. We needed nothing else.

This was our eternal paradise. To be cherished by us forevermore.

Beloved

"Jaina …" I murmured as she continued to kiss down my body.

She was still lost in the flow, ravishing me, relishing me.

"Babe, I've been thinking…"

"Hm?" she slid up and kissed me on the lips. "About what, Alex?"

I cupped her face in my hands and smiled.

"The choice I would've made, if I didn't get it all. If I had to choose between you and Stellaris, and there was no way out, I … I'd like to think I'd have chosen you, Jaina. I want to believe that I'd protect you, no matter what it cost me."

I sighed.

"Of course, I can't say I'm being truly honest here. I did go out of my way to avoid facing this possibility, so maybe musing about it is kinda hypocritical of me, isn't it?"

"Alex, it's okay. I get it, I really do."

God, Jaina's smile was so wonderful.

"I think that the reason you're thinking about this is because you're wondering how far you'd go for me. You're wondering what all you'd be willing to sacrifice for my sake."

"Yeah, that's right Jaina. I … I really, really want to believe I'd do anything for you. But I also never want to face that kind of choice again. It's just so confusing."

"Alex, neither of us can know for sure what kind of hard choices we'd make, until we face them. I can't tell you that I know you'd give up everything for me. That's simply not true."

I knew that Jaina was just being honest here. But still, hearing those words stung a little.

"But I can still make a choice. I can choose to have faith in you, even if I can't be absolutely sure. And that's what I'm doing. That's what I've been doing for so long now, ever since I fell in love with you. Whether or not you decide to save me is up to you, Alex, but regardless of what you choose, I'm placing my life in your hands."

Her arms wrapped around me, as she resumed kissing down my body.

"After all, isn't that what intimacy is all about? We bare it all for each other. We're completely exposed, completely vulnerable. Right here, right now, I'm allowing you to do whatever you want to me, just as you're allowing me to do whatever I want to you. It's such an integral aspect of making love."

That's right. How many times Jaina had been like this? Bare. Fragile. Completely cocooned in my arms.

My biggest wish was to keep her safe with me. Keep her happy. But if I wanted to, I could just as easily hurt her. Maybe even kill her. And she took that chance with me. Day after day, over and over again. Because she loved me.

And on most days, the possibility of me hurting her would never even cross her mind. She'd just take it for granted that I would hold her only to please her and warm her. It was simply a given.

And here I was, more worried about what I'd give up for my beloved when I was already giving up my own body, my own space. Opening it up completely for her to do as she pleased. All these what-ifs dogged my mind when I'd already been reaffirming my love for her all this time.

"Thank you for giving yourself up to me, my love," I said, pressing my lips into her chest. "And in return, of course, I'll give myself up to you. Do whatever you like with my body. I trust you, Jaina."

And so we surrendered ourselves to each other, as we always did. And our surrender was rewarded with joy and warmth like it always was.

Because our love had been true this entire time. And that's all that mattered.

Iron Fist

"No … no no no NO!" Royce slammed his fist onto the desk, before gazing up again, despondently, at the monitor.

It was all gone. The Rebel Network he'd relied on, and depended on, had just shut down and taken all the money with it. He should've known. He should've known it was too good to be true, but when they were all so desperate for options, how could they not be blinded to the truth?

"It really is gone, isn't it?" He heard Gemma's voice speak up from behind.

"Yeah, yeah it's gone. Our resistance is done for. Maybe we never even had a chance to begin with, but … these goddamn Coalition monsters!"

"The Stellaris Coalition? Are you sure they're the ones who did this to us?"

"Who else could it be? Who else would be vindictive enough to string us along with false hope, only to take it all away? Those people are monsters!"

"Maybe," Gemma muttered. "But then again, it's not like there's any honor among thieves. We can't just presume that everyone else resisting the Coalition would be as honorable as we are. Any number of people could've been behind it."

"I ... I don't know," Royce muttered. "Either way, we should probably evacuate this base. I don't want to take any chances. If, by any chance, the Coalition really did play us, they would've ..."

Just then, the two of them heard the sound of something getting thrown into the room. No, it wasn't just one thing ...

And then, a series of explosions knocked them off their feet. They looked up to see the entire building ablaze.

"No ... no they wouldn't. They wouldn't have ..." Royce muttered in shock, barely registering the gunfire and screams all around him.

"Royce! Royce, get up!" Gemma yelled. "Come on, we need to ..."

Suddenly, her head popped open like a melon, and she fell, dead.

He looked up to see two silhouettes, pointing their guns at him.

"Yes, he's the last one," one of them was saying.

That voice sounded familiar. Could it really be...?

"Jaina?"

The figure pointed the gun at him, and his vision blacked out. Forever.

Committed

Alex wrapped one arm around my hip as I looked over the bodies of Gemma and Royce. My two former associates at the Lightwardens, that I'd just killed with my own hands. Along with around 30 others, alongside Alex and the rest of our strike team.

We had doused the flames that had erupted due to our grenades using the special-issue fire extinguishers we had equipped. It made it easier to analyze the sites of our operations and ensure we didn't destroy too much evidence.

I turned over to Alex, and I could see the conflict bubbling in her eyes. Throughout our mission, she'd been stone-faced, stoic. But now that it was all over, I could see her softening up. She took off her helmet and looked me straight in the eye.

"Are you okay, babe?"

In response, I removed my own helmet, wrapped my arms around her, and kissed her deeply.

"I'm more than okay, Alex. I'm committed now. Committed to you, and our world. My purpose is completely, perfectly clear."

She chuckled in response, her tone betraying both relief and melancholy.

"Yeah. Yeah, this is the path I've been leading you on, ever since I met you. Ever since I spoke to you. I should've known it would always lead to this."

She caressed my cheek, her gaze full of so much warmth, and concern.

"Just ... promise me one thing. Let me be there for you, Jaina. If you have anything on your mind, anything at all, you can trust me with it. You're not my subordinate, you're not my attack dog. You're my partner, my equal. Don't ever forget that."

I kissed her again.

"I love you, Alex. And I'll always carry myself as your equal. So I'll be honest with you. The only thing I care about is ruling this world with you. That's it. For the sake of our paradise, I will do anything, but the moment I lose you, none of this will matter anymore. Loving you, finding happiness with you, and destroying anything that gets in the way of that, is what my purpose is, Alex."

"I know." She kissed me back, on my lips, on the cheek, and down my neck. "I know, my love. But I only want you to work with Stellaris of your own free will. The moment you have second thoughts, the moment you want to seek out another way, tell me. We will work it out, together."

"I will tell you, Alex. I promise. But right now, I really am happy. I really do want this."

"Okay then." Her smile was warmer now, her doubts having melted away. "As long as you're happy, we'll continue to rule this world, together."

We then got back to business, picking up the bodies of Royce and Gemma and lining them up with the other rebels we'd neutralized. We then zipped them up in body bags and tagged them for disposal.

By this time, the atmosphere in the room had relaxed, and everyone in our all-female strike time had removed their helmets. Just like Alex, they were an incredibly friendly bunch underneath their consummate professionalism. Way back in the past, such a contrast would have shocked me, even scared me, but now I could relate. I could relate quite well.

"So, you two lovebirds got quite into it once the op was over," Kara said as she approached us, her teasing, mischievous smile instantly getting me to lower my guard. "I always knew you were a couple, but you've got quite the history together, don't you?"

"Yeah, we do," Alex said. I put my hand on her shoulder and briefly nodded to get her to lower her guard.

"I was a former Lightwarden. Signed up shortly after the two of us moved in together," I said. "We've just killed several of my former associates."

"Oh." Kara raised an eyebrow. "And you didn't even bat an eye. Talk about doing a 180."

"Yeah, I suppose I did. But this new world is worth fighting for, and so I'll do what needs to be done."

"Hmm …" Kara muttered, as Beth walked in on our conversation. Kara turned to face her.

"You know, Beth, I've been wondering if you've felt the same way, but hasn't our morale been a lot better because of Jaina here?"

Beth looked at me with an approving gaze.

"Yeah, yeah I'd say it has. We've been really close to each other now, ever since we formed our new squad. It's quite remarkable."

"And did you overhear the part where she said she's a former Lightwarden, and these …" She pointed to the body bags. "These are her former associates?"

"I did." Beth's smile widened. "Go on, out with your little explanation already."

"It's as I always said," Kara said with a cocky grin, "There's no faith without doubt. The Coalition higher-ups were pretty smart to not go full 'exterminate the opposition' right off the bat. It really did give us a chance to see who among the rebels could be turned to our cause. And let me tell you, Jaina, you've been an indispensable asset. We're so, so lucky to have you!"

She suddenly grabbed me and held me in a close hug. "Relax, this is just some sisterly affection!

I mean, do you have any idea how many girls on the strike team have warmed up to you? Everyone can see what a bundle of joy you are, you know?"

"R-really …?" I muttered, embarrassed. "I never really noticed."

"Of course you didn't! You're always so wrapped up with your precious Alex. Which is cute, in its own way. But you really do have to see the bigger picture sometimes, you know."

She pulled away.

"With you around, all of us feel like a family, you know? You're such an inspiration. And I think it's because you've seen every side of this. You've been against us, and now you're with us, so your conviction and your empathy would be stronger than anyone else's. I just don't want you to ignore this gift of yours, alright?"

It truly felt quite flattering to be showered with so much praise and affection. To realize that I was so valuable not just to Alex, but her comrades, the very elite of Stellaris's forces, felt really, really good.

"Thank you, Kara. I … I won't forget this." I said, as I looked her in the eye and smiled. "If

I've really made such an impression on you all, I'll do my best to make the most of it."

"That's the spirit!" Kara said, as she affectionately patted my head. "So, I imagine none of us have any plans for the rest of the day, so how about we all go out on the town? No need to change into anything fancy, walking around in our combat gear has its own appeal, and lets everyone know who's boss. Beth?"

"Yeah, I'm up for it, if the rest of you are."

I turned to Alex.

"Hey, do you ..."

"Of course!" Alex said, with the warmest smile. "I want you to do what makes you happy, after all."

I leaned in and kissed her.

"Yeah," I whispered. "I really am happy, Alex. So, so happy."

I had figured out by now, of course, that Stellaris had always planned for complete dominance over this world. The longer anyone continued to vigorously oppose Stellaris's rule, the more brutally they'd be crushed in the end.

Those who remained resolute in their opposition, from actively targeting Stellaris property, most notably their conditioning infrastructure, to "free" the people, to actively trying to assassinate key executives, would never relent until our regime was destroyed. And so, no matter the specifics of their transgressions, they all had to die. For instance, none of us had any reason to believe that Royce or Gemma would ever order their people to kill anyone in pursuit of their aims, but I had no problem eliminating them and their team nonetheless.

And so I looked at all these beautiful girls, the elites of Stellaris's ultimate Black Ops squad that Alex and I had put together. All of them were among the chosen ones who ruled their own dimensions under Stellaris, but unlike so many who'd given themselves over to hedonism and indolence, they were all humble. Diligent. Professional.

It would be quite fair to say that our squad, more than anyone else, were the true rulers of this entire world. And they were my closest companions, people I'd do absolutely anything for.

Little by little, I had obtained not only the world itself but true comrades I could share it with.

And all of this because I chose my love for Alex over everything else in my life.

This was my reward! This was what I had earned! And I would savor it for every single day that I lived.

The Sisterhood

"That's it? Just seven?" Kara said mockingly to Diane as we sat around the table, waiting for our meals to arrive. "My record is ten times that."

"What, seventy?" I said in amazement. "How'd you manage that?"

"A few strategic advantages and some quick thinking." She smiled. "So I was on this mission in my world to destroy this smuggling operation that was slipping contaminants into the food supply, y'know, to disrupt the people's conditioning. Turns out, the materials they have to use are quite flammable. I just snuck around, planted a few charges, blew the entire place up and killed everyone inside. They never even knew I was there."

"That is amazing." Beth smiled. "I don't think anyone here could top your solo record. Well, with the exception of Alex of course."

"Yeah." Alex smiled self-effacingly.

"Yup. You launched a one-woman blitzkrieg on the final rebel stronghold in the Americas and single-handedly eliminated all 150 of them. No one's gonna surpass that," Kara chuckled.

Alex had told me about this event. It happened shortly before she'd come home from her global war for Stellaris. The remnants of various rebel factions had stockpiled supplies and ammunition, planning one major push on Stellaris HQ while their forces were spread thin. Thanks to some timely intel, Alex managed to stop them before it was too late.

I smiled eagerly as I leaned in and kissed her, making sure to drag it out as long as I could. I then faced the others and said,

"Yup. And she's MINE!"

The other girls looked at me in shock, then admiration, and finally began cheering for me ecstatically.

"Hell yeah! You go girl!"

"That's the way to do it, Jaina!"

"Woohoo!"

Alex bowed her head sheepishly, as I wrapped my arm around her shoulder.

"Kara, you said I was the one who brought up morale in this squad, didn't you?"

"Yeah, I did," she said, smiling in anticipation.

"Then how's this for a morale boost! We own this world! We run this world! We know what we want, AND WE WILL TAKE IT!"

"YEAH!" They all cheered in unison.

"WE WILL TAKE IT! WE WILL TAKE IT!"

"YEAAH!"

The wonderful jubilation lasted into the night, as we shared more stories over our meals, and I deepened my bond with all the other girls in the Black Ops squad.

Kara, of course, took to me very quickly and I was already seeing her as the little sister I never had.

Beth, beneath her soft and reserved exterior, was a surprisingly insightful woman who I managed to talk to for hours about my past, my history with Alex and my hopes for the future. She was an incredibly attentive and empathetic woman, understanding me almost as well as Alex did, just from a more platonic perspective.

And finally, Diane was really fired up thanks to my speech and just rambled on and on about how motivated she was to re-assert her dominance over her world and take whatever she wanted. I couldn't help but chuckle as I listened to her passionately go on about her hopes and dreams.

I had never in my life experienced friendships as wonderful and close as these. I would trust every one of these women with my life, no matter what happened, and I felt so much gratitude for Alex in particular for bringing me into the fold. I was so glad I joined Stellaris. I was so glad I embraced this new world.

And more than anything, I was so, so grateful for my new sisterhood. I would fight with them, and die for them, without hesitation. But more than that, I would make sure our wonderful days together never came to an end.

Triumph and Satisfaction

"Yeah, Beth, that's right, yes!" I moaned as my excitement built up, my beloved knowing only too well how to ravish me.

She didn't say another word as she diligently pleasured me, and my anticipation built up to a sweet, amazing climax as I held her tight. I wanted to feel it when she came. I wanted her joy to resonate through my body, just as mine was resonating through hers.

And sure enough, we felt each other's joy as our bodies writhed in ecstasy, the pleasure reaffirming our eternal love for each other.

"Beth," I whispered as I kissed her. "I love you. I'll give you anything you desire. Anything at all."

"I know, darling." Her smile was so sweet. So ... calming. "I know how much you love me. But it was nice getting intimate again. It's nice to have our bodies do the talking."

Our uniforms were scattered across the bedroom. God, I'd been so turned on right after our operation ended and we zipped up those rebel scum in those body bags. Truth be told, the reason I didn't want to change out of our combat gear was because I wanted to make love to Beth just as she looked when she unleashed that beautiful carnage. And I had a feeling she wanted the same thing.

"How many do you think it was between the two of us?" I murmured as I kissed down her neck.

"Hmm, probably fourteen," she murmured, "I think Alex got eight, Diane got five, and Jaina got three, including both Royce and Gemma."

I chuckled in response. "Well, I guess as a couple, we did rack the highest kills."

"That we did," Beth said, and we kissed. "I mean, Alex still got the highest count individually speaking, but I wasn't expecting Jaina to have too high a count herself. That said, she did personally kill the leaders, who were her own former associates. I'd say she's proven herself."

"That she has. Not that we had any reason to worry. I always knew Alex could turn her," I said, as I kissed down her body. "And she was so over the moon during our celebrations. Jaina's just so fascinating."

"Is that why you copped a feel when you hugged her out of nowhere?" Beth said, her tone playful yet knowing.

"Yeah, sorry about that babe. Couldn't help myself. I mean, I knew I'd get you alone eventually, but seeing someone turn so completely … I just couldn't resist that pull."

"Well, not to worry." She chuckled and kissed me on the lips. "I already got my payback."

"You did? Wait, are you talking about …?"

"Yup, our one-on-one during the celebrations. You wouldn't believe how much she opened up to me. I almost felt like I'd stolen Alex's thunder!"

"Oh yeah," I said, as I knowingly chuckled. "It's not just about physical intimacy with you, is it?"

"Yep. The emotional closeness, just peering into her heart and soul … it was a satisfactory revenge."

I buried my face in her breasts and began kissing them.

"Glad to know we're even then."

"Yeah, we're even my love," she said softly, as I continued to savor her body.

"You know," I whispered, "Even though we turned Jaina, I'm glad we're being so merciless now. I like having my resolve, my commitment tested. I like that our definition of terrorism keeps expanding, and we keep getting more and more ruthless than our enemies, killing them even when they're not trying to kill us. This ... this is what true power feels like."

"I know babe," Beth whispered back. "I'm just grateful that you can share your joy with me. You're a really, really loving woman when you're happy. And I want to make you happy, as much as I possibly can."

"Beth ... God, I love you so much. To think a consummate killer like you can be such a warm and sweet woman. I can't get enough of that contrast."

"I mean, that is true for the entire Black Ops squad, isn't it? Even you."

"Yeah, it is. But you're the one I get to explore to the fullest. You're the one I get to understand in every possible way. And maybe, through you,

I can begin to understand myself. That means so, so much to me."

"In that case, I'm glad, Kara. You can pick my brain whenever we're alone together. It makes me so happy that I'm useful to you."

"You're so much more than useful, babe. You're priceless. You're the most precious person in my life. We will rule this world side by side, no matter what happens. And if anyone gets in our way, we'll kill them and we'll celebrate their deaths by making love to each other, just like tonight."

"Yeah ..." Beth was panting now, her excitement building up, "Just like tonight."

I pleasured her with a renewed focus, eagerly anticipating the second euphoria that was to come.

The Ones Who Win

"Hello?" I said as I picked up the phone.

"Hey, Alex." I heard Gabby's voice on the other line. "How are you?"

"Oh, Gabby. Yeah, I'm doing alright, I think," I said as I snuggled back into bed. Jaina was still sleeping, her arms around me, so I shifted myself to be closer to her.

"So I got the reports last night. It seems like my little Rebel Network trick worked like a charm. Congratulations on clearing out Royce's entire cell. The pitiful resistance is only getting more and more pathetic."

"Yeah, we are having a pretty good run."

"Indeed. And it couldn't have happened without you, Alex. You have been our finest operative, leading the charge for our expansion efforts, consolidating our strength. And all the insights you gained from Jaina ... it's been invaluable in helping us understand the mindset of potential rebels, and how we might contain them. This world will bend to us, and it's all thanks to you."

"Look, Gabby, I mean it is an enticing motivational slogan and everything, but the world doesn't just bend for a few people. We're still workers for Stellaris, after all. Everything we do is to uphold that institution."

"Oh, is that hesitation I see in your voice?" Gabby said with a giggle, which somewhat annoyed me. "Come on, Alex, the whole point of upholding this system is so that we can benefit from it. Sure, technically we're simply employees carrying out our designated roles, but these designations are just a cover. We've always aimed to be the ones on top."

"What do you mean 'we'?"

"Alex, I mean me, Becca, and everyone else in our good graces. You want to know what those foolish old men on the Board of Directors are doing right now? The ones you supposedly answer to?"

"What are you talking about?"

"They're completely lost in the worlds that our system created. Their worlds aren't even grounded in reality like yours or mine, oh no. They live in full-on fantasy land, and only come out to check in once in a while about whether or not things are sustainable. And I show them that their little dream world is still being paid for and they go back."

"So, out of all of Stellaris senior management, you and Becca are the only ones doing any managing?"

"Now, don't sell yourself short, Alex. That's where you and your Black Ops squad come in. Did you ever wonder why I granted you access to every single world we have once I briefed you on our system? It's so that you could lead the efforts to secure and monitor them. You think I know every little detail of what goes on in each of our chosen ones' domains? No, that's the job of the automated monitoring systems you put in. And you're the one who knows best how they work."

"I … I'd always thought those orders came from the top. I thought I was doing this for the Coalition …"

"See, that's the problem with you, Alex. You have all these defense mechanisms, these stories in your head that you use to protect yourself from realizing how powerful you really are. And it's been endearing, it really has. But it's about time you grew up and faced reality. Everyone knows what's what. Even Jaina. So why are you hesitating?"

"Gabby ..." my voice hardened, "Just what are you getting at?"

"Oh, I don't mean to threaten you, if that's what you're thinking," she said. "Like I said, I've given you enough insurance against me if my ego ever gets the better of me. What I'm trying to explain to you is that there's a reason I chose you to be the check against me and Becca. There's a reason why you have enough power and leverage to direct this world however you want. And that reason has nothing to do with your sense of duty towards Stellaris. The Board and their petty agendas can rot for all I care. Stellaris is nothing but a means to an end."

"Gabby, I've never claimed to have any love for the Board, but all this talk about Stellaris being a means to an end? Are you saying that this whole time I've been fighting for nothing?"

"Alex, there's only one reason to amass this level of power. To subjugate so many people, to create a system that benefits us at their expense. It's because we're the only ones worthy of steering civilization. Me, Becca, you, Jaina. Don't you see? Stellaris isn't some inscrutable behemoth that's bigger than you. Stellaris is your tool. It is your weapon. And I trust you with it more than I trust anyone else."

"What are you saying? Is this just some pep-talk to butter me up? To inflate my ego?"

"Again, you're retreating, Alex. Trying to tell yourself that you don't have to be responsible, that you don't have to be the leader. But you're worthy of this. You upended the bigoted legacy of your Vander lineage and became the first queer woman to lead the family. You have won over the masses, time and time again, no matter how much blood we spilled during our expansion efforts. The people in your and Jaina's world are so peaceful, so content. And Jaina changed her entire value system for you. Everyone wants you to rule over them, Alex. They want you to guide them."

"So, what? You want me to shape not just my world, but every world in my image, because you think I'm the most worthy?"

"Yes, Alex! Yes! All Stellaris does is provide you a cover story, and a set of tools you can use to make your life easier. I'm not telling you to take everything on your shoulders and give up the happy life you have now. But I do want you to acknowledge who you really are. You're the greatest accomplishment Stellaris has ever had, you're the lynchpin of our continued success and prosperity. You're the one Becca and I are entrusting everything to because when you win, we all win! And you need to rise from your self-effacing shell and own it!"

"Gabby, I …" I was at a loss for words. I'd been taken aback by Gabby's fervent admiration of me, but now that I thought about it, she wasn't lying in the slightest. It really did seem that the further I went in my service to Stellaris, the more of the world seemed to fall into my hands. Our economic dominance. The chosen ones who had their own worlds to rule. The masses who were forcibly conditioned to obey us, defer to us. And I had reaped the rewards of all of it.

And I was the one being trusted to keep this system afloat. To ensure that people like me, Gabby and Becca continued to reign supreme, no matter what. Because I'd been good at it. And I'd been generously rewarded for my efforts.

"Yeah, you're right," I said. "I … I've been too good at hiding. From myself, from the truth, from my own power and responsibility. I appreciate everything you've said, about my worthiness, about your faith in me. I won't forget it."

"Awesome!" Gabby squealed in delight. "I'm so glad I got through to you! Never forget how proud I am of you, Alex. Never forget how proud we all are! I'll just leave you to think over matters in private now. I'm confident you'll shine brighter than ever before. Love you."

She hung up.

I put down my phone and looked over at Jaina. She was still asleep. Still smiling, her arms wrapped around me. She shifted her body a little and pulled me closer.

When we'd first gotten together, she'd lamented so much about the state of the world. How corporations like Stellaris enriched themselves at the expense of the masses, how she wanted to make a better world for the powerless among us.

And I'd pushed back with my stubbornness and seduced her with my reassurances. I promised her that everything would work out, that one day she'd appreciate what Stellaris was doing.

So Jaina resigned herself to the state of the world and eventually embraced it. She began to relish the comforts and luxuries I provided her, and she joined Stellaris, and me, in defending the world as it stood. Even if it meant gunning down the very rebels she used to work with, find common ground with.

And all this while, I never gave the masses any real power. I subjugated more and more people to Stellaris's rule, and ultimately took their very free will away from them, in the name of peace. In the name of stability. No matter what I might have told Jaina, or even myself in the past, this was the world I'd been working towards. This was the world I'd created. And I'd done such a good job at it, I was the one being entrusted over everyone else to make sure things stayed the way they are.

My beloved was sleeping so peacefully right beside me. But a part of her was as good as dead now. Because I killed it, even if it was with kindness.

I could no longer deny it. This was who I was. This was what I wanted. And the only thing that made me sad was knowing that if the Jaina of old saw me as I was now, she'd have never fallen in love with me. It was only through the lies I told to both her and myself, that I was able to get my happily ever after.

I wrapped my arms around her, bringing my body closer until I could feel the warmth of her skin. Her breath.

"But still, there was one thing I never lied about," I whispered. "I did want you to be happy. I really did consider you my princess."

Yes. All the moments we had together, of peering into each other's hearts, understanding each other, creating our universe together long before Stellaris came in with all their talk of dimensional layering and mind control, holding her as she was crying and wondering if she'd gone crazy, her reassuring me that she would give up anything for me, me wanting so desperately to make a world worthy of her.

All that couldn't have been a lie, could it?

"I need you," I whispered to her, as my voice cracked and tears streamed down my face. "I need you, I need you, I need you, I need you."

I held her closer, my arms wrapped as tightly as they could be. Jaina moaned sleepily but didn't wake up.

"I need you. You're everything to me. Everything. Everything …"

And so I whispered through my tears, begging her for salvation that would never arrive. Because why would she ever absolve me of anything? She already loved me, already accepted me. She was perfectly happy with the life she shared with me.

And as for her older self, who would disdain me and chastise me for what I'd done, why, I'd already destroyed her with my charms, my honeyed words, with a love that suffocated her until she was nowhere to be found.

So who was it, exactly, that needed to forgive me?

"It's all for you, babe. Everything. I just want you to be happy, that's all. I just want you to be happy."

My hands were shaking as I held on to her, the pain in my heart refusing to subside, the desperation wracking my body refusing to fade. And there was no one left who could understand this.

Or was there?

"Hey." I heard her whisper, as her lips kissed me on the cheek.

"Jaina?"

Her eyes were open now, and she was smiling. Not a cheery, over-the-moon smile. A quiet, understanding smile. A comforting smile.

She kissed me on the lips again, then whispered,

"I understand, babe. I understand everything."

"Jaina … my love … I …"

"I forgive you, Alex. I forgive you for failing. I forgive you for not creating a world worthy of my ideals. I forgive it all."

"I … I …"

"I forgive you for placing your own happiness over that of the world. I forgive you for making promises you couldn't keep. I forgive you for your part in convincing me that the welfare of the masses wasn't that important after all."

"I'm sorry …" I said, as my sadness gave way to relief. I couldn't believe it. There really was someone to listen to me after all.

"I just … feel like I've built everything on lies … that I don't deserve you at all!"

"Alex, it doesn't matter what you say, what you think. I still love you, I'll always love you. Always."

"If you'd seen this side of me back then … there's no way … there's no way you'd ever …"

"Alex, I did see this side of you. I did see you hurt people. You even hurt me. And all the times you kept telling me things would get better, I could tell that you didn't really want to change the course of the world. You simply wanted to keep me happy. So that's the choice I made, that I would be happy in the world you were making. Because I love you."

"I … I really did change you so, so much."

"You're not the only one responsible for that. I let you influence me. I let you comfort me. I let you turn me. I am not your victim, Alex. I was never your victim. And I'm sorry I ever let you think that way. Forgive me."

"Jaina, there's nothing to forgive …"

"But there is," she said, her voice firm. "It was too easy for me to believe that I was changing for you. That I forsook my old ideals for you. It was quite comforting even. It made me feel more selfless, more noble than I really was. But I see now how much that lie has hurt you, so I need to face up to the truth. I changed because I wanted to change, Alex. I gave up my old ideals because I was happier without them. I embraced this world because I grew to like it. You're not the only one keeping things the way they are, I am too."

"Jaina …"

She gently kissed me on the lips again, and said,

"And that's why I need you to forgive me. For all the pain I caused you by allowing you to assume responsibility for my choices, my decisions. For letting you think that you killed a part of me that I'd willingly thrown away. For letting you believe that I was some pure-hearted angel you had to protect."

"Jaina … oh Jaina …"

I held her close and kissed down her neck.

"I forgive you. I forgive you for all the ways you hurt and manipulated me. I forgive it all. I … I've always loved every part of you. I've loved it when you've been happy with me, when you've indulged in my gifts, and enjoyed this world. But I've also loved your idealism, your desire for things to be better, your expectations for me to be better. And I can't have it all at once, and some parts of you change at the expense of others, and I can't help but wonder if I'm somehow letting you down, babe. Because that's all I'm afraid of, letting you down."

"I know, my love. I know. So promise me one thing, okay?"

"Yeah, Jaina?"

"Next time you feel this pain, this fear, I want you to grab hold of me, take me away, and let it all out. No matter where we are or what we're doing."

Her hands caressed my cheek.

"I want you to open your heart to me whenever it's hurting. I want you to trust me with your most fragile moments, your darkest thoughts, your most desperate desires. I want all of it, Alex, so whenever it bubbles up, let me have it."

"Will you ... promise the same to me, Jaina?"

In response, she smiled and kissed me. Slowly, deeply.

"Yes, my love. I promise you. You will have my heart whenever it's in pain. You will have all my fears, needs and desires. After all, you're the love of my life, Alex."

Relief washed over me as I heard those words. Just how did she know? How did she sense that I was in need, and how did she know exactly what to say, and what to ask?

No, perhaps I was putting her on a pedestal again. Perhaps, if the situation was reversed, I'd have done the same thing. I'd certainly like to believe that was true.

And as I looked at Jaina, smiling at me, cocooned in my arms, I realized that I would be happy in any world where I could have this moment.

Home

I signed the final papers and handed them over. With this, the orphanage I'd started up would become a formal Stellaris academy. It felt strange to close the last stretch of distance I'd kept between myself and this company. I'd already given away my present to them. Now, I'd signed away the future too.

Not that I was regretful. This was what I needed to do, after all, to prove to Alex that I was responsible for my decisions. That I was just as complicit in Stellaris's actions as she was. That we weren't equals only in name.

I took her hand as we started on our way back home. We didn't say anything to each other. We'd save it for when we'd returned.

And soon after we returned home and put down our purses, I turned around and wrapped my arms around her.

"I love you," I whispered as I kissed her on the lips. Again, and again.

"I love you too, Jaina. I love you more than anything else," she whispered back.

Our bodies were yearning for more, and slowly we gave in to our urges. But while I did want to make love to her again, I wanted even more to affirm her. To treasure her.

Even if my body would inevitably please her and satisfy her, I wanted her to cherish her moments with me because she'd remember how precious she was. How invaluable she was. How irreplaceable she was.

"I can't imagine living without you anymore, you know? I've devoted so much of myself to making you happy … if you went away, I don't know what my purpose would be," I murmured as I slowly undressed her.

"I feel the same way, Jaina. I'd be lost without you too. But still ..." She smiled sweetly as she kissed me. "I want you to be happy no matter what, not just for my sake. If you can live a wonderful life regardless of what becomes of me, I'll know that I was part of something bigger than myself. I want to do something for this world that doesn't just work for my benefit."

She gently pushed me down and slowly fondled my body.

"Everything about you is distinct. Separate from me. And it should be. You should be your own person, not an extension of my will. Your light, your freedom, it's something I wish I'd never shackled. I wish you could've been yourself every time you've been with me. But even if I wasn't perfect, even if I did change you, I want you to be free."

"I don't know, Alex. I just feel so focused when I'm living for your sake. If I just think about how to make you happy, how to do right by you, I'm comfortable. I'm at peace."

"I get it, my love." She continued to kiss my body. "The temptation of being controlled is just as sweet as the temptation of being in control. And as long as you want me to guide you, and take care of you, I will. But that's not the life I want for you. Not because you're a burden to me, but because there's so, so much more to life."

She kissed me deeply, fiercely, the increasing aggression in her lovemaking betraying the softness with which she still spoke.

"I promise you, I will put my life on the line to make sure no one ever shackles you. I will protect you even if I have to turn against this very world I created. I have accomplished everything I ever set out to do, Jaina, but all this power and adulation will mean nothing if I can't stand by you."

I could feel the pressure on my body rising. I could feel her passion, her longing, testing me. Even as she whispered such honeyed words, her body was testing my resolve. My desire to be free.

I squirmed in discomfort, unwilling to push back. I felt so tired, thinking about everything. How the world had changed, how I'd let it change, how Alex had changed me, dominated me, and yet she was telling me she didn't want to keep things that way? Why not?

Why couldn't she just keep it simple?

What was so wrong with just wanting to spend my days asleep in her arms?

She kept saying there was so much more to life, but I was just overwhelmed now. It tired me to think, to contemplate, to look ahead. Why couldn't I just lose myself in her love? What was so wrong about that?

Her lips were on mine as she kissed me fiercely, relentlessly, still testing me. Still analyzing me.

"Trust me, Jaina, you haven't fulfilled your destiny yet. You still have so much ahead of you."

Why should I care though? Why should I want anything more than what I already have? If I was happy and comfortable, and at peace, why should I change anything?

"Alex, I …" I tried to formulate a response, but I just couldn't put it into words. What could I even say?

In response, she simply smiled and kissed me again, and slowed down the pressure she was putting on me.

"You're tired, aren't you? It's alright, I'll be gentle now."

Yes, this felt safer. Less overwhelming. This was what I wanted Alex to be right now. My comfort. My sanctuary.

"Jaina …" she murmured, as I felt my arousal build up. "I like it when you talk to me, Jaina. I like the sound of your voice, the passion with which you talk about your dreams, your fantasies, your ideals. I love getting lost in the stories you tell me. I'll be so, so happy if you could keep doing that."

"You like it when I talk to you?" I murmured.

"Yeah. It can be about anything. Even if you're not making any sense, just hearing your voice makes me happy. So you can say anything to me, Jaina. Anything at all."

"I … I want your body Alex. I want to feel that sweetness, that rush. I want you to be the one who pleases me. Just you. I only have eyes for you. My precious knight in shining armor. The way you smile at me, talk to me, I can't get enough of that. I feel satisfied every night, and the next day I want more. I want you to be mine, Alex. All mine! Mine alone! Give me … give me … aaaah!"

I moaned with joy as I felt the sweet euphoria wash over me. Yes, this is what I wanted from Alex. I wanted her to please my body, cherish my body. And only her. No one else. Not one other person would ever have the luxury of loving me, of exploring me, like she did.

"And, if you want me to be free, if you think there's more to life, I … I still don't want to live it without you. I don't want you gone, Alex. Please, just stay by my side forever. There's no one else who can. There's no one else I want to love."

"I understand, Jaina. I hear you. And I will always listen to you. No matter what you say. So just keep talking, alright?"

"Did you enjoy it too, Alex? Did you feel my love too?"

"Absolutely, babe. Absolutely. And I will only belong to you, no matter what, alright?"

"Okay." I was so relieved. So, so relieved. "I want you, and me to..."

My stories blended into one another. The next morning, I couldn't even remember most of what I'd said. And I was fine with that because I remembered something much more important.

That my beloved Alex was by my side the entire time.

Paradise

"So I hope you understand now why the Coalition is necessary," I said to the people facing me.

They all nodded. I wasn't sure how many had been convinced by my words, and how many were simply acquiescing because they saw no other choice. Either way, I'd accomplished my objective.

After all the months I'd spent with Alex and my squad crushing rebellions through force, I was making the last of them surrender through my words. The words of someone they could relate to, by virtue of my opposition to Stellaris in the past.

"They surrender," I spoke into my earpiece. "You can move in."

And so the security team moved in and handcuffed everyone. They were subsequently escorted into a van and driven off.

I took out my phone and texted Alex.

"It's done."

As I returned home and rang the doorbell, she answered and immediately took me into her arms.

"Hey, babe," she whispered as we kissed.

"Hey, Alex." I looked into her eyes and smiled.

She ushered me in as I hastily took off my shoes.

She took me to our bed, plopped me down, and continued kissing and fondling me from above.

"So it's over?" she whispered as she slowly, gently undressed me.

"Yeah. Those were the last rebels I know of."

"Okay," she murmured. "I'll have you withdrawn from the black ops detail then. You've done enough for Stellaris, Jaina. Now it's time for you to live for yourself."

"Are you sure? I don't want to make any trouble for you, Alex. If they want to keep me on, I can stay."

"No," she said, her tone firm. "You've proven yourself, Jaina. Many times over. They have no right to keep you under their thumb."

"Alex, it's fine. I'm not doing this because I have to, I just ..."

Alex immediately silenced me with a kiss.

"You're doing this for me, aren't you?" she whispered.

"Y-yeah ..."

"Then let me pay you back, Jaina. Let me reward you. What's the point of us accumulating all this power if we can't use it for ourselves?"

"Alex ... serving you ... serving your dream is what gives me purpose. It's what drives me day after day. I'm happy with that."

"I know, my love. I know." She kissed me on the lips, then down my body as she slowly peeled off my blouse. "And you've made my dreams come true beautifully. You've gone far, far beyond what I ever wanted to ask of you. You have nothing more to prove to me. Nothing at all."

"But still, if I can help you, I want to!"

"But so do I, Jaina!" Alex said, raising her voice. I could sense some anguish and frustration building up in her tone. "I can't have you just endlessly chasing after mine or Stellaris's approval for the rest of your life! You used to have your own dreams, didn't you? Your own aspirations? Why do you keep pushing them away, Jaina? Is it ... is it simply impossible for you to pursue those dreams anymore? Is following me and Stellaris all you have left?"

I could sense the fear behind her question. I could feel her lingering guilt from all the times she'd coaxed me, pressured me into putting her aspirations before mine. Despite my reassurances, despite my forgiveness, it still ate away at her. Even now, she couldn't shake the feeling that she'd made me lose myself.

She was still thinking about the old me, who'd pushed back on her ideals. The old me, who was far too naïve and idealistic to accept the world she'd been so determined to build. The old me that I'd left behind for her sake, but she still couldn't let go of.

My poor, poor Alex. She just couldn't bring herself to forget the woman she'd fallen in love with in the first place, even though that woman no longer existed.

I did not know of any other way to answer her question, aside from brutal honesty.

"Alex ..." I murmured. "It's true. Following you is all I care about now. I want to be the best lover, the best partner, and the best friend you could possibly have. And other than that, there's not much I care about. And as long as you're loyal to Stellaris, I want to keep serving them. As long as their vision and yours align, my purpose lies in enforcing their will. Any prior ideals of mine that conflicted with this ... are ideals I've abandoned, forever."

"Jaina ..." she whispered, continuing to kiss down my body. "I'm not asking you to go back to opposing Stellaris. I mean, I guess I do miss that side of you, but I'm not naïve. I know something had to give. I just ... want to do something for you too. If I'm the only one taking the lead in our relationship, I'll start feeling like I'm just using you to satisfy my desires. I'll feel like I've reduced you to my personal outlet. And I find that disgusting ... I could never forgive myself for treating you that way. So please, give me something to do for you. Just take the lead, Jaina ... I'm begging you."

"Hmm …" I murmured, lost in thought.

She was still caressing me, still peppering me with kisses. Slowly. Gently.

"You've called me your princess, haven't you, Alex?"

"Yeah," she smiled wistfully. "You're my princess, and I'm your knight."

"Then how about we go back to working on our kingdom? We can reopen the scrapbook and start talking about our own universe again. You can escape all your obligations, all your commitments, and go back to creating that world that is ours and ours alone."

"Yeah, yeah we can do that, my love. I'd love to do that."

"Yeah, Alex. Let's keep building that universe. If you agree to that, I'm fine with you withdrawing me from the black ops squad."

"Yeah, yeah that's just what I wanted to hear, my love!" she said, sounding utterly overjoyed and relieved. And I could feel her relax as she started pleasuring me in earnest.

"Alex, I love you so, so much!" I whispered. "So come with me whenever you have the time. Come with me to our universe. We'll keep building it, bit by bit, until we have the perfect paradise. And we'll be the only ones in it."

"Yeah, baby. A universe, just for us. It'll be so beautiful. So, so beautiful. I love you, Jaina! I love you I love you I love you!"

"Oh, Alex! I love you! I love you! I LOVE YOU!"

I screamed as the ecstasy took over me, her love filling my body, my very soul, with such euphoria.

My precious, precious Alex. I loved her more than anything else in this world.

Making Memories

"Wow!" Beth smiled as she looked at the drawing on the scrapbook. "You're a really good artist, Jaina!"

"Actually," I smiled. "That one isn't mine. That's all Alex."

"Really?" Kara said, amazed. "She's come that far? You must be one hell of a teacher, Jaina."

"That she is," Alex said as she smiled at me and leaned in for a kiss.

God, it felt so gratifying to be so open about our love.

"I'm jealous now," Kara said. "You two are such hardcore romantics. I thought Beth and I were super-indulgent, but this is something else."

We'd started painting our dreams into a scrapbook. Our wildest fantasies, our most indulgent desires. But that had quickly evolved into something else. Alex and I also started another scrapbook, that chronicled our history. Our journey together.

Our deepest thoughts were for us alone. But this commemoration of what we meant to each other was what we were showing to Kara and Beth.

"Relax," Alex said. "Everyone loves in their own way. We're not trying to one-up you, you know."

"I know, I'm just teasing." Kara giggled. "Beth and I are very happy together, I assure you."

"But still, looking at all this, I'm kinda glad you withdrew from the black ops work." Beth said, "This really is so beautiful. Superior might can only go so far in stabilizing society. The people need something more. Something to celebrate. Not that you're obligated to make a spectacle of yourselves, I'm just thinking out loud!" she said, a sudden nervousness overcoming her.

"It's alright," I said. "You're just thinking of the big picture. I get that."

"Yeah, I mean, look, I just want you two to be happy." She grinned sheepishly. "Whether that means continuing the Stellaris Coalition's work, or just enjoying the fruits of your labor, people like you two deserve to be happy."

"Aw!" Kara said and immediately kissed Beth. "You're so adorable, you know that?"

"Kara, don't embarrass me!"

"Too late!" she said and continued to kiss her.

"Dammit, now you're making a spectacle of things! Not that I mind ..." she murmured.

After a few moments of indulgent affection, they turned their attention back to us.

"You know, even though we obviously can't go out on ops anymore, it's nice for you to invite us over," Kara said. "You really didn't have to stay in touch after you left, so this is appreciated."

"Come on, you two are practically family to me. Black ops or no, I want us to remain the best of friends for the rest of our lives!" I said.

"Yeah, you made that very clear. We'll be sure to stop by whenever we're free," Beth said.

"And I know you both have leaned on me a lot as you learned the ropes, and I don't want to just put a stop to that," Alex said. "I'm always here to lend an ear."

"Oh Alex, that's just like you, you know. You're so strong, and kind, you're my hero!" Kara said and pulled her in for a hug. I didn't mind.

"Yeah, of course, Kara. I'm right here for you, anytime you need me," Alex said. She was such an amazing person. So caring. So beautiful.

The sheer joy and gratitude I felt living the life she'd brought me into wasn't something I could've pictured in my wildest dreams.

Just by meeting the right person, my life had become beautiful in ways I could never have imagined.

"Alex …" I whispered. "I love you."

She didn't hear me. She was still preoccupied with Kara. But that didn't matter. I'd already shown her my love so many times. And I would do so again. Very, very soon.

After we finished our dinner date, and Kara and Beth went on their way, I took the lead. Tonight, I'd be the one in control, no matter what it took.

"Wow … you've gotten a whole lot stronger, Jaina."

"I'm flattered," I said as I continued to feel her up. "I've been waiting for the day I could overpower you."

My grip was firm. My pleasuring relentless. I was hungry, and I would not stop until I'd had my way.

Alex couldn't escape my grasp no matter how she tried. And as that realization dawned on her, I saw her smile with so much pride.

"You're strong, Jaina. You're so, so strong. I'm really proud of you. I love you so much!"

I pushed down on her and continued to ravish her. But I hadn't ignored her words.

"I love you too," I said, my soft reply contrasting with the sheer intensity of my lovemaking.

But that's the woman I wanted her to see me as. Soft-spoken, demure and loving. But with a hidden strength that could never be underestimated. This version of me was the reward she deserved for all the love she'd showered me with, time after time. I was being strong, being powerful, for her.

"I'm taking you, Alex. You will be mine tonight."

"Yeah. I will be. Jaina … I love you …"

Her body was just as sweet as always when I dominated her. And her faint whispers of gratitude were ones I would remember as among my fondest memories.

Strategic Romance

"Yeah, Kara. Go on, go on ..."

I eagerly pleasured Beth as she whispered to me, my passion only growing stronger as I relished her body. Her touch. Her voice.

"I love you, oh, how I love you ..." I murmured while doing my best to show it.

She was so precious. So very, very precious. And I was so, so lucky to be the love of her life.

"Yes my love, yes, oh yes!" she murmured, and I knew that the euphoria had seized her. Her arms wrapped around me and tightened their grip as she eagerly sought to return my favor.

And so I too felt that wonderful sweetness, and the immense joy that could only come from knowing that she was happy too. I surrendered myself to the pleasure, to her warmth, to this amazing moment, and drowned myself in its bliss.

"Mmm ..." I murmured, caressing her and kissing down her body, still intoxicated from the afterglow.

She too was murmuring, the happiness in her voice unmistakable.

"I never want to stop doing this ..." I whispered. "I never want these days to end."

"And they won't," Beth replied. "We're the chosen ones, Kara. We're the inheritors of this world. We've made it bend for our happiness, and we'll keep doing that, for all eternity."

"Yeah, an eternity of moments like these ... to think I was so fortunate ..." I caressed her face. "This is everything to me, Beth. You are everything to me."

Yes, this world belonged to us, and we'd never let anyone else lay claim to it. We'd exhaust every resource, work every last commoner to death, and drain this world of all life before we let anything take us apart.

But of course, it wouldn't come to that. We were already in a wonderful equilibrium, with the chosen among us getting everything we desired, while the masses below labored to serve us, whether they knew it or not, whether they wanted to or not. And if this ever stopped being sustainable, we had so many options. Cryogenic preservation, a mass culling and population reset, heck, even the Coalition's space exploration efforts were starting to bear fruit. When we finally figured out how to colonize new worlds, this planet and its people would have at last outlived their usefulness.

As I continued to savor my beloved, these ruminations faded from my mind, as I relished in the simple pleasures of her touch, her lips, and her warmth.

And just as we were settling down, ready to tuck in and embark on the world of dreams together, I heard the phone ring.

"Why now?" I lightly grumbled as I took my cell phone from the bedside. "Hello?" I said, taking the call.

"Hey, Kara. Sorry it took so long for me to check in. I've been a little caught up." I heard Gabby say.

"Nothing too serious, I hope?"

"No, it wasn't anything problematic. Just … tedious," she sighed. "So anyway, how was Jaina acting today? Her and Alex still stable?"

"Yep, they seem very comfortable staying with Stellaris these days. I really don't consider Jaina a security risk anymore."

"I see. Any idea what they plan to do after withdrawing from their Black Ops duties?"

"Hmm … I think they're happy to just spend their days together and take on whatever passion project strikes them. They really seem to be into making artwork these days. Very intriguing."

"Alright. And just to be clear, you didn't find any seditionist material?"

"Nope. I did a thorough inventory while Beth distracted them, but they're completely clean as far as I'm concerned."

"Okay, then." There was a pause on the line, and when Gabby spoke again, she was notably more relaxed and perked up. "It seems our strategic encouragement of their love affair has been a resounding success."

"Now, don't give me too much credit. This was mostly yours and Becca's idea." I chuckled. "Beth and I only stepped in after Jaina had formally joined Stellaris, after all."

"That's true, but your monitoring has been crucial in helping us track the progress of our little experiment. Despite our fears of the project backfiring, and Alex potentially rebelling against us at Jaina's behest, it turns out we never really did have anything to worry about."

"Yeah, I don't blame you. I mean, I agree that a healthy romantic relationship is critical to enhancing people's sense of belonging and their strength of will, but that can easily work against you if they turn on you. But personally, I think it came down to Alex's loyalty to our cause. Despite the reservations she may have developed under Jaina's influence, I could tell that she'd never want to turn against us if she could help it."

"Yes, Becca and I felt the same way, which was why we encouraged her to want it all. That way, we'd get all the benefits of her being romantically attached, with none of the downsides. And I'm happy to see things have turned out so well."

"Yeah, so am I. It's good to see how Jaina finally recognized her place was among the elites like us, not the lowly masses who weren't worth saving anyway. And Alex's main concern was doing right by Jaina, so I think that problem solves itself."

“Well, that part is a little more complicated. I think Alex may have become somewhat uncomfortable about Jaina losing so much of her rebellious streak, so we’ll have to make sure she doesn’t obsess over it too much. To that end, I hope you and Beth remain close to them and provide the appropriate guidance so that they can find satisfaction and fulfilment as the elites of this world.”

“Don’t worry, we’ll keep working on them. I don’t think it’ll be that hard. After all, they already consider us friends. They’ll listen to us.”

“I know they will. I just wanted you to be clear on what the stakes were. You and Beth have been indispensable to this project’s success.”

“Thank you, that … that means a lot,” I said, with a smile. “We’ll keep doing our best.”

“Becca and I know you will,” she said. The warmth in her tone made me feel so happy. “And one last thing. I want to reduce the frequency of your reports to just once in two months. We can’t have Alex or Jaina suspect that they’re under surveillance, so nothing you do should appear out of the ordinary.”

“Understood, ma’am. I don’t think they’ll ever find out, but even if they do, I think we can leverage Alex's sense of duty, or Jaina's concern for Alex's safety, to prevent matters from escalating."

"Yes, that is a good insight. Thank you for everything you've done for Stellaris, Kara. Gabby out." she said and hung up.

I crawled back into bed and snuggled against Beth.

"Hm, that was a long call." she said.

"Indeed it was." I smiled and wrapped my hands around her, eager to savor her body again.

"I love you, Kara. I love you so, so much."

"I know, darling. I love you too." I murmured.

And so we enjoyed each other once more until the dreams came to take us away.

Temptation Fulfilled

"I know what you're trying to do, Beth." I said, looking her in the eye.

"What do you mean, Jaina? I was just trying to …"

"I know you've been watching me. Monitoring me. Monitoring Alex. Don't bother trying to deny it."

She went silent for a moment, before sighing in resignation.

"Okay, I won't. Kara and I were tasked with investigating you for any ulterior motives, seditionist activities, you get the idea. We were just covering our bases, you know. Our Coalition didn't get this far without taking the proper precautions. You do understand that, right?"

"I do," I said solemnly. "I suppose the ways I've changed might have appeared too good to be true for people like you. And I don't know if I'd be here if it wasn't for Alex. But I want this life, Beth. I'm not throwing it away for any reason."

"I know, Jaina, but ..."

"Of course, you know. You've been spying on me, after all."

"Yes, yes I have. But it was nothing personal, really. Kara and I have nothing against you. We want you to be happy."

"So long as I stay loyal to Stellaris, right?"

"Y ... yeah."

"Well, like I said, I'm not throwing this life away. I'll be happy to keep working for Stellaris for the rest of my life. It's the best solution for me, for Alex. For all of us, really."

"Yeah, it is. But I just want you to know, Jaina, my friendship with you, how much I care about you, it's not a lie! It was never a lie, it's just ..."

"It's conditional, right?" I smiled. "I don't mind, really. I know that you and Kara think differently about things. We were never going to completely see eye to eye. But I still like you, Beth. We can still be friends."

"Oh, Jaina ..." She smiled with relief and put her hand on my shoulder. "That's such a relief to hear. And not just because of my duties to Stellaris. I ... I genuinely feel bad about breaking your trust like this. I'm going to talk things over with Kara. We're not going to keep any more secrets."

"That's good to hear, Beth. And just so you know, I'm not going to doubt you either. You're still my best friend."

In response, Beth closed the distance between us and pulled me in for an embrace.

"Thank you." Her voice was breaking. "Thank you, Jaina. I'll ... I'll find some way to make it up to you. I'll make things right."

"You don't have to. This is just another price I had to pay for being in Alex's world. Being mistrusted, being watched, none of it surprises me. But I've always hoped things would work out eventually, and it looks like they have."

"I still don't understand it, you know. Why would you give up so much to join us? If I was in your position, I don't know if I would've gone this far. It'd just feel like I let the enemy win."

"It's simple. It's because Alex was the perfect temptress. She let me embrace my vices, my sins, and gave me a chance to make all my dreams come true. Not just the noble ones I clung to in order to convince myself I was a good person, but other dreams as well. Dreams I would've never faced, much less accepted if I hadn't found her."

"Hmm … so you want the same things as us, then? The power? The supremacy?"

"Yeah. I want to be rich. I want to be powerful. I want to be important. And I care far more about Alex than I could ever care about the masses I thought I had to fight for. Now that I have her, I longer feel compelled to try to be this good person who does everything right. I no longer feel like I have to fix anything. Because I gave in, Beth. I gave into her love."

"That … that sounds oddly beautiful."

"Because it is. Being led astray by her is the best thing that ever happened to me. It made me understand that there is no path I ever have to follow other than my own. People can say what they want to say. They can praise me, or condemn me. But the power to choose is mine, and mine alone, and nothing can ever change that."

"I envy you, you know. No matter what, you'll always have her. Whether you stay with us or turn against us, she'll never, ever leave you. You're so free, Jaina. If only ..."

"If only you were as well?" I smiled as I looked her in the eye. "Are you sure Kara wouldn't stand by you no matter what? Don't you think she'd always protect you with everything she had, no matter what you did?"

"I ... maybe, but ..."

"You've just been too afraid to ask, haven't you? I get that. But I believe in her, you know. I think she would say yes if you asked."

Beth sighed in relief as her grip upon me loosened.

"Yeah, yeah you're right. I need to believe in Kara too. Thank you for this, Jaina. I ... this was more than I deserved from you."

"No it isn't," I said, firmly. "We're friends, and friends look out for each other."

"Yeah." She smiled. It was such a beautiful smile. "Yeah, they do."

Beth quickly turned around and headed to Kara, who'd just finished her conversation with Alex. I watched them for a few moments, as Beth aired out her insecurities.

And just as I'd hoped, Kara smiled, held her close, and kissed her.

"I'll always love you, always. We'll finish this conversation later, alright?" she said.

"Yeah, we will," Beth murmured. "Jaina was right. I'm so glad she was right."

Alex looked over to me, her eyebrow raised. I waved her over so we could talk on our own and give Kara and Beth some privacy.

"Seems like you and Beth had a lot to discuss," she said. "How are you feeling?"

"I'm feeling amazing!" I said and eagerly kissed her. "Thank you, Alex. Thank you, for everything."

"Well, you're welcome. And thank you, Jaina. Just being around you makes me feel like we're going to be okay, no matter what happens."

"That's because it's true, my love." I kissed her again. "I know we'll always be together. And because of that, we can face anything."

"Yeah. Yeah, we can." she said.

And she smiled. And she looked so happy, so grateful. And she was smiling at me.

This was what I lived for. This was what I looked forward to every single day. And the life I'd live would be full of moments like these, over and over again. I just knew it would.

The world had changed so much. I had changed so much. And things would change again, whether for the better or the worse.

But I knew that nothing would ever keep Alex and me apart for long. Because we had created a universe for ourselves, which would always be waiting for us.

Always, and forever.

Thoughtform surveillance: Final Report

OVERSEERS: REBECCA BURNS AND GABRIELLA ADAMS

SUBJECTS: ALEX VANDER AND JAINA MARSHALL (ORIGINAL), KARA HAYWOOD AND BETH ROBERTS (ADDITIONAL)

LOYALTY TO COALITION: "EXEMPLARY" GRADE FOR KARA HAYWOOD AND BETH ROBERTS, "PER EXPECTATIONS" GRADE FOR ALEX VANDER, "WITHIN SAFE PARAMETERS" GRADE FOR JAINA MARSHALL

COALITION STRENGTH AND SECURITY: ALL FOUR ARE INVALUABLE ASSETS TO MAINTAINING AND CONSOLIDATING COALITION CONTROL. RECOMMEND RETAINING FULL AUTONOMY FOR ALL SUBJECTS AND LEVEL 2 SECURITY CLEARANCE TO COALITION RESOURCES.

POPULATION RESOURCE MAINTENANCE: POPULATION CONTROL, POPULATION EXPLOITATION, POPULATION SURVEILLANCE AND DISSIDENT SUPPRESSION TO BE CONTINUED BY KARA HAYWOOD AND BETH ROBERTS.

PERMANENTLY WITHDRAW ALEX VANDER AND JAINA MARSHALL FROM ACTIVE DUTY AND REASSIGN TO ADVISORY ROLES. THE PEACEFUL DOMINANCE OF THE COALITION FACES NO IMMINENT THREATS, THEREFORE OPERATIONS AT BASELINE READINESS ARE RECOMMENDED.

FINAL SUMMARY AND RECOMMENDATION: ALL FOUR SUBJECTS ARE INCREDIBLY VALUABLE AND TRUSTED ASSETS OF THE COALITION. THEIR INDEPENDENCE AND COMPLETE AUTONOMY ARE INSEPARABLE FROM THEIR UTILITY, AND THEREFORE THEY SHOULD BE ADEQUATELY REWARDED PER OUR VOLUNTARY SERVICE GUIDELINES TO ENSURE LONG-TERM COOPERATION. THOUGHTFORM ANALYSIS HAS AFFIRMED THEIR LOYALTY, ALONG WITH A CAPACITY FOR INNOVATIVE THINKING NOT POSSIBLE WITH MENTALLY CONDITIONED SUBJECTS.

WE RECOMMEND CEASING ALL SURVEILLANCE AND CANCELLING ALL CONTINGENCY PLANS REGARDING EMERGENCY CONDITIONING. SUBJECTS SHOULD OPERATE FREELY AND

INDEPENDENTLY WITH NO EXTERNAL INTERVENTION AS LONG AS PRESENT CIRCUMSTANCES PREVAIL.

END REPORT

www.ingramcontent.com/pod-product-compliance
Lightning Source LLC
La Vergne TN
LVHW041146150826
845673LV00001B/86

* 9 7 9 8 8 9 0 6 7 6 0 3 0 *